# Reformation

A story of common people living in the
early years of the Protestant Church

**Nathan Driscoll**

malcolm down
PUBLISHING

First published 2024 by Malcolm Down Publishing Ltd.
www.malcolmdown.co.uk

25 24 23 22    7 6 5 4 3 2 1

British Library Cataloguing in Publication Data
A catalogue record for this book is available from the British Library.

ISBN 978-1-915046-87-1

Cover design by Esther Kotecha
Art direction by Sarah Grace

Printed in the UK

# Dedication

To Malcolm and Mary Deall

My close friend, Malcolm, combined his deep faith with an equally profound understanding of the human condition. His compassion for others never waned. Malcolm and Mary made a huge difference in many people's lives.

# Contents

# Acknowledgements

As ever, my wife, Jenny, has been supportive, encouraging, and has helped me develop the story and respond to advice. Her subtle ideas have helped me to open up the story in the light of my research into the history of the time. My friend Tim Edwards has offered his help generously, as he has done for all of my previous publications. His deep knowledge of literature, time and thoroughness is always offered in a gentle and constructive way.

Sincere thanks to my publisher, Malcolm Down, once again for giving me the opportunity to write this story. He is always encouraging and supportive. I also want to thank Sheila Jacobs for her editorial guidance, particularly in making me realise that stories should not simply be vehicles for revealing the history but should stand up in their own right. For the artwork my thanks go to Esther Kotecha and Sarah Grace, for their clear and striking ideas.

# The Trigger

Along with everyone else, for nearly two years I have watched and read about the shattered lives of ordinary people caught up in the war in Ukraine, and more recently in Israel and Gaza. For innocent people going about their daily business their already fragile lives are then torn asunder by pain, poverty, cruelty and death.

Trying to compel people to switch their national allegiance, as Russia has attempted to do in Ukraine, creates deep and lasting resentments. The attack by Hamas on Israel in October 2023 involving mass murder and the taking of hostages has, at the time of writing, led to the whole population of Gaza being denied water, food and fuel, with many places reduced to rubble and strewn with corpses. The intensity of the conflict is volcanic; perhaps by the time this comes to press the situation may have quietened, but hatred can lie dormant. In such extreme situations the leaders of each side naturally justify their own actions and condemn their opponent's claims. Each side claims to be telling the truth while the enemy is lying. Controlling the 'mindset' in war is all part of the battle.

I decided to explore how the control of the 'mindset' worked in the sixteenth century at the time of the Reformation. Would there be any similarities between what was happening then with the events of today? Did the people choose their faith as individuals, or was it chosen for them by their rulers? When the ruler changed, did the religious practice and beliefs of the people also change? How did those in power balance their own self-interest against those they represented? How much choice did ordinary people have in the way they lived their lives?[1]

---

1. I have listed the main sources I used at the end of the book, and also provided a brief summary of the historical background and aftermath of the story.

To help me explore some of those questions, I read about the history of the period and then created a fictional story based around that history. This book is that story. I, of course, hope that it is compelling and sheds light on how intently the Church's and State's actions affected the lives of the common people. I have tried to be faithful to the outlook of the historical characters such as Luther, Melanchthon, Zwingli and Bucer (men of the Church) and political leaders such as Frederick of Saxony and Philip of Hesse. References to the Holy Roman Emperor, Charles V, and the practices of the Roman Church are also based on the information I gathered. The other characters are fictional.

# Location

The main action in the story begins in a very small area where the principalities of Saxony and Hesse met. Schmalkalden is the main town where the Town Council is based. The council retains authority over the neighbouring villages, including Rotterode Abbey and Bermbach Monastery. The principality of Palatinate, to the south, is relevant in the second part of the story.

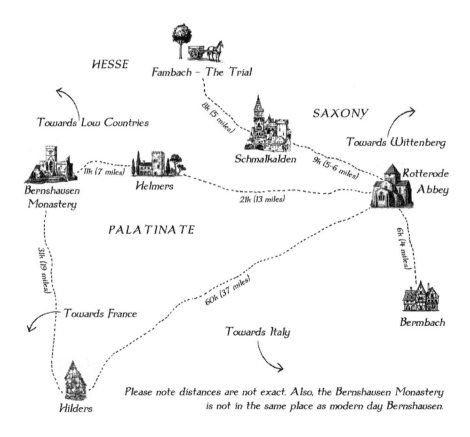

HESSE

Fambach – The Trial

Towards Low Countries

SAXONY

Towards Wittenberg

8k (5 miles)

9k (5-6 miles)

Schmalkalden

Rotterode Abbey

11k (7 miles)

Helmers

Bernshausen Monastery

21k (13 miles)

PALATINATE

6k (4 miles)

31k (19 miles)

60k (37 miles)

Bermbach

Towards France

Towards Italy

Hilders

Please note distances are not exact. Also, the Bernshausen Monastery is not in the same place as modern day Bernshausen.

# The Setting

Medieval village life all over Europe was based on the Lord of the Manor's authority. Disputes over the use of small strips of ground, straying animals and weak ale were commonplace. Fines could be levied for the non-payment of death dues, marriage taxes or failure to carry out work on the Lord's land, known as the demesne. A tenant would always have to organise harvesting his own crops outside of his obligations to work on the manorial land, or risk being fined. The bailiff was the Lord's chief officer; his continuing presence ensured that the Lord's crops and stock were properly looked after and that as little as possible was stolen. He would purchase such items as building materials, parchment, utensils and thatch from local markets and organise the provision of food for the labour force when they were required to work on the demesne.

Most people were unable to read, more so outside the cities. However, those who became Priests or Sisters were literate, as they were taught the Vulgate, the Latin Bible. Everyone was connected to the Church and payments of money and of goods to the Church were deeply tied up with fears of avoiding purgatory, a halfway house between mortal death and the everlasting fires of hell. The Reformation brought a new edge to an already downtrodden and precarious life.

Whether you were a serf working for the Lord of the Manor, a tenant farmer or a labourer, your life and that of your family was always in the balance. A fear of poor harvests, sudden rent increases, the arrival of soldiers plundering your crops and mistreating the women and the threat of disease were ever present. Your pottage made from barley and oats washed down with water, or weak ale if you were lucky, would keep you from starvation; the main and preoccupying purpose of life for many was to stay alive.

# PART 1

## The Death of a Priest

# 1

# West Saxony:
# Autumn 1543 – a Forest Walk

Creeping through the night-time forest, Sister Mary tripped over a root; stunned by the fall, she momentarily thought about turning back towards her ruined abbey. She had set off an hour or so after the soldiers had left. Picking herself up she said to herself, 'I have to go on.' She began to pray in broken words, 'Lord ... please ... Lord ... mercy ... grace ..' She was speaking each word as she took each uneven step. Intermittent shafts of moonlight sparkled through the treetops as she peered through the changing spectrum of twigs, branches and undergrowth. At times it was very dark; such slow going, and sunrise was several hours away. Sister Mary had to get to the monastery to tell them the news: Brother Wilhem was dead. She was soaked to the skin and still in shock from the sheer brutality of the attack. Her eyes, normally clear and bright, felt like closing as she tried to remember the way in the darkness; all the landmarks in daylight looked so different, and her fear rose instantly when the wolves howled.

Brother Wilhem had been conducting the weekly Mass for the Sisters. He was a quietly spoken man, devout and always willing to walk the seven miles between his monastery and the abbey, even when his left leg pained him from the muscle-wasting he had begun to endure. Now his long body lay speared on top of the altar with the communion wine poured over him and the bread stuffed into his mouth. The gory image was in Sister Mary's mind as she fixed her eyes on the forest floor, damp with rain. The treetops which danced in daylight seemed to taunt her small frame. Her leather water bottle had split open in the fall, and she had eaten the two slices of bread she had left the abbey with. How long would it take?

Finally, she was banging at the front door of the monastery at Bermbach using a broken branch found nearby; it was four in the morning. She waited.

On the other side of the door, Brother Helmold felt certain who it was; he recognised the beat of the knocking. 'One of the usual beggars,' he thought.

'You know you must come for bread and soup at eleven o'clock, don't you?' he said firmly through the door, and began to walk back towards the cloisters, where he and the other Brothers would pray silently every morning before the first formal service of the day at six o'clock.

'No, no, it's Sister Mary!' she cried out, plaintively. 'Brother Wilhem has been killed by Philip of Hesse's soldiers while taking our Mass – you must open the door! I have walked here through the night on my own – the others were too shaken to come. Please, please help me. He has not even been given the last rites. How could they deprive him of that? Why has God allowed such a despicable act? Tell our Holy Father to come and hear me, I beg you. The soldiers will come back again.'

Brother Helmold stopped and listened; retracing his steps, he opened the door. 'Sit here,' he said to Sister Mary, keeping his hood up. Immediately he went to look for Father Hermann, the abbot.

Father Hermann was still asleep when Brother Helmold knocked at his door; his house was set apart from the monastery itself.

'What is it?' he mumbled, half-awake now. He heard Brother Helmold shouting. Father Hermann was hard of hearing and the thick wooden door did not help. But eventually he understood what Brother Helmold was saying: 'Brother Wilhem is dead!'

He shuffled to the door and it opened with a creak. The abbot absorbed the news without a word. Despite being full of indignation, a strange thought occurred to him; had he been in Brother Wilhelm's shoes, he would perhaps be thought of as a martyr. That might be preferable to what he feared most, the coming destruction of his monastery by the Protestant soldiers. He went back inside to put his robe on and hobbled as quickly as he could to the main courtyard. He composed himself in case his emotions got the better of him, for he still wanted to appear in control.

Sister Mary looked up to see Father Hermann's portly figure and thinning tonsure facing her. She was still crying. He waited. At first, every sentence was punctuated with sobbing but gradually she was able to talk.

'We were about to take Mass when the soldiers burst in … shouting, "The Pope is evil . . . we are the Schmalkaldic League, God's own soldiers!" Some surrounded Brother Wilhem and others started to destroy our blessed icons and precious statues … they broke them and laughed … I heard someone say, "Claus, that's enough … leave it now … we have made the point!' They pushed us Sisters aside and spat on the floor as they left … we were terrified and then we looked to the altar . . . there he was, blood streaming down his side, just like our Lord at Calvary … and they had desecrated the Mass!'

Sister Mary broke down again and could not continue.

She was given some food, dry robes and a room to rest in but she could not sleep; desperately grasping for comfort she found none and stared vacantly at the wall, breathing audibly with her whole body. She steeled herself to pray but she had no words.

Father Hermann was inwardly distraught but he had a whole set of immediate problems to solve. Before doing anything, he called four of the senior Brothers and held a Mass in memory of Brother Wilhem. Afterwards he retired to his own room and the questions began to flow into his mind. How would they bury Brother Wilhem, even though he had not had his last rites administered? How would they carry him the seven miles back and find suitable holy ground? And where would that be? How could he ensure that the grave would not be discovered and despoiled by the Protestant soldiers? He eventually called for the senior friars to come back to his house, ordering the servants to bring food and wine. They prayed for the saints to protect Brother Wilhem's soul from a lengthy spell in purgatory. After some intense discussion, each of the senior friars went back to organise the recovery of the body and the funeral Mass.

After dark that same evening, ten Brothers arrived at the abbey near Rotterode where the killing had taken place. The Sisters, at the behest of Sister Margarete, the abbess, had already laid out Brother Wilhem in a small room adjoining the abbey church. It had taken eight of them to carry him away from the altar where he had died. The abbess had then asked the Sisters to leave her alone for a while as she quietly wept over Brother Wilhem. Rising to leave and making sure no one saw her, she had turned round and gently kissed him.

The Brothers carried him out silently on a roughly made wooden stretcher and said nothing for the few hours as they trudged on, occasionally stumbling with the weight on their shoulders. It was slow going, with some of the more able-bodied Sisters following behind with water, bread and dumplings. Every hour they would stop to refresh themselves. The six miles took them all night and a few more hours; they did not bring him as far as the monastery grounds, as that might attract an unwanted visit from Philip of Hesse's men.

A grave under the trees had been prepared, just a mile or so away from the monastery. Sister Mary had stayed there, to recover, but joined them now. It was the middle of the afternoon; Father Hermann prayed over the ground, swinging incense as he spoke out words of judgement on the murderers. He dedicated the ground to the Almighty, throwing wild flowers into the grave.

Earlier, Sister Mary had told Father Hermann what Brother Wilhem's last words had been: 'Pray, Sisters, that my sacrifice and yours may be acceptable to God, the almighty Father.'

Father Hermann repeated those words and went on: 'The sacrifice Brother Wilhem spoke of was the bread and the wine prepared at the altar to be changed into the body and blood of Christ during the Eucharist. Instead, Brother Wilhem became the sacrifice himself. He stood at the altar before God while the devil's soldiers filled the church, destroying the statues of the Holy Mother Mary and ripping down the sacred crosses. Brother Wilhem tried to stop them, but they crowded round him. As they ran out laughing, he lay there on the altar, motionless, brutally murdered. As God is my judge, may they be brought to justice, both here on earth, in purgatory and in the raging fires of the eternal hell prepared for them.'

His eyes bulged in rage and he almost fell over. The Brothers and Sisters stood in silence as he went on to recite a passage from Lamentations:

> Remember, Lord, what has happened to us;
> look, and see our disgrace.
> Our inheritance has been turned over to strangers,
> our homes to foreigners.
> We have become fatherless,
> our mothers are widows.
> We must buy the water we drink;
> our wood can be had only at a price.
> Those who pursue us are at our heels;
> we are weary and find no rest.[2]

2. Lamentations 5:1-5, NIV.

After the apostolic pardon was recited and Father Hermann took the Mass, Brother Wilhem was laid to rest. The grave was covered over with branches and twigs. One of the Brothers climbed a nearby tree and hammered in a small cross high up. A small piece of wood was also nailed there. It said in very small writing:

Brother Wilhem died at the hands of bloodthirsty men. May his soul be saved through the arms of Our Lady into eternal life with our Lord and Saviour, Jesus Christ.

Father Hermann suddenly stopped in his tracks, his rage still there. 'No!' he boomed. 'Are we ashamed? Let Brother Wilhelm's grave be marked with a large cross. He gave his life for His Lord and Saviour and the Holy Mother.'

Quietly weeping, the Sisters returned to the abbey and the Brothers to the monastery. Two of the younger Brothers returned soon after with a heavy cross, which was planted firmly at the head of the grave. Creeping into the abbey in the early hours, the Sisters knew their world was no longer theirs. What would happen to their lives? Would the villagers stop providing them with milk and cheese? Would they even be able to look after the children during the harvest, when all the women had to go into the fields? How would they survive without the weekly indulgence payments given by the villagers as penance? When would the soldiers come back – as they surely would?

# 2

# The Tavern – Three Days Later

The tavern was a mile or so away from the barracks on the outskirts of Schmalkalden. The soldiers, both mercenaries, called *landsknechts*, and local young men recently recruited into the Protestant army, approached the large, ramshackle building. They had just been paid and were in high spirits. The afternoon light softened as they sauntered along, and the young locals felt self-conscious in the company of the older, battle-hardened campaigners. The smell of roasting meat from the kitchen was in the air as they approached the tavern.

The wooden tables were scattered around and the publican's three big dogs ambled about, sniffing and growling. When he called them for their food they instantly went, each eating only from their own bowl. The story of two men who had refused to pay for their drinks, laughing as they left, was something the publican made sure any new customers were aware of; the dogs had nearly cost them their lives before he had called them off.

There were six women in the kitchen and four working girls who were under the strict control of Hette, the publican's wife. The four girls would serve the beer until their services were required upstairs; if they were all engaged, the men would have to collect their drinks and food from the counter; most evenings by nine o'clock the four girls were nowhere to be seen. The better-off local tenant farmers had an understanding that if one of them paid for time with one of the working girls, the others would not tell the man's wife, especially if the harvest was poor and food was in short supply.

Stephan and Claus, two of the *landsknechts*, walked in along with Michael and Tobias, two young locals who had recently signed up.

Philip of Hesse and Frederick of Saxony had, for the last year, levied additional taxes on the common people to pay for the new Protestant army. No one quite knew if Charles V, the Holy Roman Emperor, would turn his attention from resisting incursions from Islamic invaders to regaining the German principalities for the Church of Rome. Michael and Tobias had joined to help pay for those extra taxes, leaving their parents and younger siblings to work the land. For their parents, it would be fewer mouths to feed and some of their wages might even help with the additional tax burden.

The four of them sat around the table. Claus and Stephan looked comfortable, Michael and Tobias less so. They had begun to feel a sense of unease at despoiling the Church they had grown up in.

'Did you mean to kill him, Claus?' Michael asked.

Claus laughed. 'I am a professional soldier; if you hire and pay me, then expect a trophy. A wounded friar can still speak; a dead friar tells you through the icy fear of his dead eyes who is to be feared most. I do my job well. Did you not hear Philip, Landgrave of Hesse? He wants us here to squeeze out the threat of a Catholic backlash. God wants us to obey the authorities, and that is what I do; I work for the ruler who pays the best. That is how God tells me which ruler to work for and which ruler is doing his bidding. In Spain the pay is lower and the emperor's battles are never-ending. I am doing God's will whether I kill friars, Jews, Anabaptists or reformers. I kill for God, just like King David, who slayed Goliath and the Philistines.'

Claus drank up his tankard and went over to a woman in the corner. She had been intermittently catching his eye and slowly lifting her skirt as he smirked. He reached into his pocket and drew out some coins.

'Come,' she said, 'and let's see what Gezel can delight you with.' He gave her the coins, which she handed to Hette, the publican's wife, and they went upstairs.

'One hour only!' Hette shouted out to them.

Claus shouted back, 'I will pay for fifteen minutes – we don't get paid again for another three weeks. I like to spread my pleasures out. I will be able to come back and drink more of your beer.'

The other three, Stephan, Michael and Tobias, just sat and drank their strong ale.

Tobias had a quizzical expression on his face.

Stephan looked at him. 'What's the matter?'

Tobias took a large swig and said, 'I wonder if Gezel knows she is about to pleasure the man who has just killed her father.'

Stephan laughed. 'That's a good joke, Tobias. You are joking, aren't you?'

'Buy me another tankard and I might tell you – if there is time before Gezel comes down for her next customer.'

Stephan smiled, ordered the drinks and sat down. 'Well, then? Hurry, because I am next in the queue.'

'My mother told me all this,' said Tobias. 'One day, when I was small, a girl came to stay with one of the villeins[3] living on the Manor fields nearby. The villein was Albert and his wife was Gude. The baby was Gude's niece and everyone was told that her parents had died. She was put to work at the youngest possible age. When she was about four or five, she was made to carry water and dung while the other children in the family played. By the time she was twelve, her face was full of misery. Eventually she ran away with a passing traveller, who had his way with her and left her here at the tavern. The publican, Bertold, said she could sleep in the outhouse, but he also liked the look of her. After Hette found out, he had to take the brunt of his wife's anger. Bertold got Hette drunk one evening and persuaded her that Gezel could earn them some money. Hette agreed she could stay as a working girl, provided her husband kept his hands off her.'

---

3. Tenants.

He was about to say more when Claus returned and said, 'Stephan, your turn; I need a drink.' He went over to Hette, who gave him two coins back.

Two hours later, the soldiers walked back to their camp, where they remained waiting for orders.

The next evening, round the fire, Stephan reminded Tobias that he had never finished his story. Tobias negotiated the promise of another beer and continued freely, as Claus was asleep in his tent.

'Albert, the villein who had taken Gezel in as a baby, died about five years ago. At the funeral his wife's sister, Margarete, the abbess, came, and Brother Wilhem took the Mass. The story goes that the villein's widow, Gude, saw Brother Wilhem's profile against the setting sun and in a flash realised that the angular nose, together with the slightly receding chin, was the same as Gezel's. The two women started arguing and the widow was heard to say that her sister, Margarete, and Brother Wilhem had really killed her husband, for the burden of the extra child had shortened his life. Once he heard his name spoken about in anger, Brother Wilhem left straightaway. The two women stopped arguing but it was too late; my mother told me that Sister Margarete had been Brother Wilhem's concubine when she was young. Most of the Brothers had them, anyway. After Gezel was born, Margarete's parents told her she would have to join Holy Orders and stop consorting with Brother Wilhem . . . Now you owe me two beers, Stephan.'

Stephan warmed his hands. 'One drink only; don't push your luck. What do I care, anyway?'

Claus could not believe it when visiting the tavern the next day Hette came up and told him he could have any other girl except Gezel. Demanding to know why, she retorted, 'Are you the only one who hasn't heard the story about Brother Wilhem? You may not have known it, but you killed her father. We do not want any Catholic soldiers who hear the story burning our tavern down.'

'Ha! What is that to me? Most of the emperor's soldiers are fighting in Spain anyway. And when did your tavern become a monastery? As if that makes any difference; God uses *landsknechts* like me to carry out the orders of his rulers – does he not want me to relax when I have punished such wrongdoers on his behalf?' Claus looked at Hette, but she was not finished yet.

'Did your mother and father have their last rites given to them by a priest, Claus?' she asked. He nodded. 'Then you will have to pay double for Gezel, and she will pay the extra as an indulgence for her father, as your spear pierced him and your hands stuffed the bread and wine into his mouth. Be careful – for doing that with the bread and the wine, you could become a wanted man.'

Claus screwed up his face, and shook his head. 'That's tavern talk. No one would give evidence against me. In any case, I did not kill him; he ran onto my spear in the heat of the moment and stuffed the bread and the wine down his own throat, saying we were blaspheming against the Holy Spirit. I will pay double, but just this once, so you can protect yourself from those imaginary Catholic soldiers who are nowhere to be seen.'

When he went upstairs with Gezel, he told her he had not realised she was Brother Wilhem's child and was sorry for her that he died in the scramble; he made a point of saying that Brother Wilhem had run onto his spear, but clearly Gezel had heard a different story on the tavern grapevine.

'Do you think I care?' she retorted. 'I was abandoned and then used as a workhorse by Albert and Gude. But God will punish me, as Brother Wilhem's daughter, if I do not pay an indulgence as penance for him because he did not have his last rites spoken before he died.'

Claus turned his back on Gezel as he began to undress and said, 'There will be enough money to pay the indulgence.'

Hette pushed open the battered door of the abbey; she had a feeling that giving her dues to the Holy Roman Church might matter in the future. Gezel waited outside and would not go in; she had told Hette that for the last five years, ever since she found out from the talk in the tavern, she had felt nothing for her mother. Hette was shown in to Sister Margarete, the abbess.

'Why have you come here?' Sister Margarete asked her. 'Is it to give the soldiers who come to your tavern information about us? They have already desecrated our place of worship and broken our sacred images. The villagers have stopped coming here and no longer give us milk and vegetables. They do not even ask for our prayers and help with their children. What do you want?'

Hette was no stranger to confrontation. 'Sister Margarete, you are Gezel's mother. She is outside and will not come in; that is why I am here. Brother Wilhem was killed without receiving his last rites. Gezel does not want to be sent to purgatory because her father was killed in such a way. She knows that paying an indulgence to the Church will absolve her of this. I also want it known that our tavern has helped in this way. I have no other business here.'

Sister Margarete took the indulgence from Hette and looked away. It seemed to Hette that she wanted to say something, but could not.

As Hette walked down a cloister on her way out, she turned to look into the main part of the abbey. She saw the broken icons left where they had been smashed. Some of the Sisters knelt praying before a headless statue of the Holy Mother.

Once Hette had left, taking Gezel with her, Sister Margarete retired back to her room. Two hours later she called Sister Mary. She asked her to visit Brother Wilhem's grave the next day and bury a letter near to where he was buried. This is what Sister Margarete had written:

Father God, Holy Mother and our Saviour Jesus Christ

I sinned against you many years ago and you have now wrought your punishment on Brother Wilhem and our abbey. Please, if you can, forgive and take him into your presence and accept the indulgence that his daughter has provided. If you wish me to take purgatory on his behalf, let me do so; there was no opportunity for him to have his last rites as he strove to protect the sacred image of you, O Holy Mother. Lord God on high, place your judgement on the men who blasphemed against the Holy Spirit by touching and brutalising the blessed bread and wine. May they depart to the eternal flames.

The rest of my life will be my penance.

Sitting alone inside the cold stone walls of her room, Sister Margarete thought about why her father had told her to visit Brother Wilhelm when she was a young woman. Had some promise been made to him that God would look on the family with mercy if she became his concubine? Was that the only solution? Her only duty now was to banish the memory of her intimacy with Brother Wilhelm and dedicate her remaining days to the service of God through prayer and penance. She could not push away the sadness from her soul, and quietly sat down to write another letter. In that letter she laid out her last wish, to be buried alongside Brother Wilhem. She sealed the letter and placed it on a shelf where she kept her personal belongings: a lace handkerchief her mother had given to her when she entered Holy Orders, and a small splinter of wood that Brother Wilhem had told her was found near the cross of our Lord. Sister Margarete did not allow herself to doubt Brother Wilhem's word.

# 3

# Two Letters

Sister Mary left early the next morning. The sunlight was shining through the branches as she set out for Brother Wilhem's grave. She felt a strange sense of peace as the light made the colours of the leaves brighten, and the carpet of the forest floor smelt good; what a contrast from the night after the attack. The three hours it took to get there seemed much less. She wondered what might be in the letter and why it was sealed.

As she came into the opening she stopped in her tracks; a notice had been staked to the cross where Brother Wilhem was buried.

THE MURDERER MUST SURRENDER
OR
BROTHER WILHEM WILL SPEND ETERNITY
IN PURGATORY

The tranquillity was no more and suddenly a feeling of someone else's presence descended on her. The rustling leaves conveyed a sense of fear. She wanted to bury the letter and leave as soon as she could; she began to breathe rapidly. The shadows suddenly became human and then, in a moment, just shadows again. She found a sharp stone to dig the hole and used her hands to push the earth back. She buried the letter.

As she walked away, she thought she saw a brown tunic moving behind the trees, and as she reached the open path back towards the abbey, she began to walk more quickly.

'Wait, Sister!' a voice called out, and there was a friar in a ragged, dirty brown robe behind her.

'Who are you?' Sister Mary said. 'Have you been following me?'

'I came to find Brother Wilhem's resting place. I heard how he had been cut down, and as I was leaving I saw your figure in the trees. I am a Franciscan friar, originally from the Torgau Monastery. Our monastery was destroyed by the reformers nearly twenty years ago, and for many years I lived a vagrant's life, walking miles from monastery to monastery; what befell Brother Wilhem is not new. We beg for bread and many of the Brothers are ill. But for the last six months some brothers at Bernshausen have taken me in. My name is Brother Ditmar.'

Brother Ditmar was around forty years old, gaunt from near starvation, and slightly bent over –but his eyes were fierce. He stood a respectful distance away from Sister Mary, as if he did not wish to threaten her, sensing her apprehension.

'Did you put that message there?' Sister Mary asked him.

'No, but I am glad of it,' he replied. 'Whoever speared him should hang from the executioner's rope, but to desecrate the body and blood of our Lord deserves the hottest flames of hell and more. I am not the only one who knows about the manner of Brother Wilhem's death.'

Sister Mary waited for Brother Ditmar's fury to subside a little before she spoke again.

'What troubles you more, your own sins or the sins of others?'

'My guilt is more than the weight of the cross itself – I punish myself for the sake of our Holy Mother and our Saviour, and I do that willingly, but God's wrath will overflow against those who try to prevent the likes of me from trying to avenge Brother Wilhelm's death... and you? You speak as if you forgive, or even excuse, Brother Wilhem's murderer? Do you not feel any anger?'

Sister Mary stood for a few moments, knowing that there was something in Brother Ditmar's soul that made her feel uncomfortable, even though she had some sympathy with his words. Her submissive demeanour was hiding a steely resolve.

'Our Holy Father, Paul III, has given his blessing to the Society of Jesus. I take my lead from them – preaching God's Word and acts of charity must go hand in hand. That is how we are to serve our Holy Mother, our Saviour and the Lord God, whatever the circumstances. The Lord God on high will see fit to judge as he pleases. Who am I to act as judge? Brother Wilhem's murderer will have to account for his actions, yes, in killing Brother Wilhem and in desecrating the Mass; the Lord God will deal with him according to his righteousness, not mine.'

Brother Ditmar did not soften. 'If our earthly rulers administer false justice, should we simply accept it and wait for the Lord's final judgement?'

She replied quietly but firmly, 'Our rulers should exercise justice properly, but I am not here to take vengeance, just as our Lord told the disciple in the garden to put the sword away.[4] The burden of such a responsibility would be too great for me.'

Sister Mary sensed that Brother Ditmar wanted to continue, but she desired to bring the conversation to a close.

'You must go on your way,' she told him. 'I have to return to the abbey.'

As Sister Mary walked home in the autumn glaze, the image of Brother Ditmar came back to her; what would happen next? Would he be plotting some kind of revenge? Was there even a plan to lure the murderer back into the church and then kill him? Was Brother Ditmar capable of that? She arrived back at the abbey in time for evening prayer. She wanted to lay the burdens on her heart at the foot of the cross and before the Holy Mother. She felt dryness in her throat as she

---

4. See Matthew 26:52.

looked towards the altar; the broken images of the Holy Mother and the crucifixes were at the back of the abbey covered up with woollen blankets. It was bare. Inside the cold stonework, the evening prayers echoed; there were no consoling physical artefacts.

The remaining Sisters left the abbey after the service, but Sister Mary stayed kneeling.

'Sister Mary!'

Sister Margarete's voice trembled as she hobbled down the aisle, stopping once to wipe her tears away. She paused to compose herself.

'Did you bury the letter in Brother Wilhem's grave?' she asked.

'Yes, Sister,' Sister Mary replied, wondering whether she should tell her about meeting Brother Ditmar. She hesitated, catching the abbess' eyes, sunken in sorrow and guilt. Sister Margarete's prayers were always heavily laden with regret, which Sister Mary had never quite been able to fathom, having arrived at the abbey only five years before. She was also never quite sure why she preferred the title 'Sister ' to 'Mother'.

'Thank the Lord, above,' Sister Margarete replied, but added, 'Did anyone see you?'

Sister Mary had no choice but to tell her about her conversation with Brother Ditmar. Sister Margarete's relieved expression returned to her usual dour misery.

After a few seconds, the abbess spoke again. 'We have almost no food and milk left. I have let you all down; my sins have brought God's judgement on our abbey, and I have no one to confess my sins to. Perhaps I never will.'

With that, she turned around and hobbled out.


Back in her house, she gently lowered herself into a kneeling position, knowing that she would have difficulty in getting up. After half an hour, she struggled to stand, hanging on to her table where she wrote letters from time to time. She now wrote to a living person.

Bürgermeister of Schmalkalden Town Council

Dear Bürgermeister Herr von Kram,

As you will know, our abbey was visited by the soldiers from the Schmalkaldic League and Brother Wilhem, who was taking Mass for the nuns, was killed. There are nine Sisters who remain at the abbey. The villagers have stopped coming here, and we have stopped caring for their young children while the tenants and their wives work in the fields. The usual exchange of food and penance has suddenly ceased, and I am concerned that the fields cannot be properly prepared for the winter and the animals cared for under these circumstances.

You will also know that the statues of our Holy Mother have been despoiled and representations of the saints have been damaged. I understand that you are mindful of the interests of Frederick, Elector of Saxony, and Philip, Landgrave of Hesse, but I wish to beg for your influence in maintaining peace in this manor, and re-establishing the normal exchange of services between the abbey and the local people, who are duty-bound to pay their rents and provide a proportion of their produce to you. I seek your mercy for both the welfare of your tenants and the Sisters who I have responsibility to God for. I simply ask you this: should your villeins and their families, and my Sisters, be suffering over this?

Please look on us all with mercy.

Sister Margarete

Once more, Sister Mary was delivering a letter. She had been chosen to deliver this letter on the basis of her bravery in delivering the first one. It took her nearly three hours to walk from the abbey to

Bürgermeister Herr von Kram's house on the edge of Schmalkalden. As she walked past the tenants, wives and children she knew so well from previous times on the rough, stony path close to the abbey, she did not know if she should greet them. She looked into a field where two heavy oxen were pulling a plough, preparing the ground for winter. She instantly recognised Johan and Hans, tenant farmers, in their ragged, coarse tunics and battered hole-ridden boots. All she received in reply to her look were two furtive glances. Sister Mary knew that Johan's wife was due to give birth and may have even done so, but she could not ask.

The blacksmith and the carpenter were on a corner talking to one another, and as Sister Mary passed them, they gave her a half-smile but seemed too nervous to say anything.

'What are you doing here?' said a young girl as Sister Mary walked a little further. The girl ran up to her, but a call from the kitchen of the peasant house nearby immediately made the girl stop, then run back through the squawking chickens and scrawny goats in the yard.

Sister Mary heard the mother scold the girl: 'You know you are not to speak to the nuns any more!'

'Yes, but it's Sister Mary,' the girl replied.

'Enough!' said the mother, 'or do you want the strap from your father?'

Silence followed. Sister Mary carried on for two hours, eventually climbing the short hill to the door of the Bürgermeister's house. She knocked and waited, and knocked again. A servant came to the door and Sister Mary asked her to give the letter from Sister Margarete to Bürgermeister Herr von Kram. Sister Mary turned and almost ran down the hill, taking a circuitous route back to the abbey.

Two days later, five men arrived at the abbey. They brought some milk, bread, bacon and apples. After speaking to Sister Margarete, they cleared away all the statues of the Virgin Mary and crucifixes from inside the abbey; they painted out the windows and threw the broken bits of statue and wood behind the outer wall of the abbey, giving orders that no one should touch it. They would be returning to take it all away.

After evening prayer that day, Sister Margarete spoke to the nuns.

'The Schmalkalden Town Council has ordered that our abbey be used for the common people to worship here on Sunday coming. We will attend the service, but sit at the back of the church. The Bürgermeister Herr von Kram will attend and bring a preacher of his choice. The service will not be conducted in Latin but in German, and there will be no Mass until the following week when the pastor will give communion in both kinds to the people.'

All the questions the Sisters had remained unsaid, for they knew that Sister Margarete's authority was already compromised. She had given way for the sake of being able to supply them with bread and milk. They retired for evening prayer.

# 4

# The Service

Early on Sunday, the Sisters swept the church and gathered up the leaves from the pathways inside the abbey walls. The local Lord of the Manor, Herr Herland Schulz, had made it known that he would be attending, and word got around. The villagers and their children did their best to make their ragged clothes look smart, making sure their torn sleeves were hidden inside their moth-eaten coats; some even kept one or two items aside for the Sabbath, perhaps a hat, or a fresh tunic, or a pair of boots.

The publican and his wife also came; Gezel and some of the other girls followed. Times were uncertain and the slightest deviation from the expected could bring on trouble; Hette was taking no chances. The common folk automatically knew where they should sit, and held a respectful silence as a few of the merchants from Schmalkalden entered with their wives to sit in the first few rows. They dressed in velvet-lined cloaks and grey hats, but it was their semi-stiffened faces that told everyone how important they were. Unlike their wives, with their dresses flowing down from gathered-in waists, the men ostentatiously removed their headwear as they entered the church.

Sister Margarete and the nine nuns sat at the back. In among the crowd was Ditmar, and with him was another Franciscan friar. With the church nearly full, five or six guards appeared as Herr von Kram, the Bürgermeister of Schmalkalden Town Council, came in, placing himself in the first row. Space had been left, but his glance told the town councillors to hurriedly shift sideways to create more room. He had decided to employ a Protestant preacher for the sake of maintaining social order in the countryside surrounding Schmalkalden where the Protestant Military Defence soldiers were based.

Behind Herr von Kram came a man wearing a black robe which parted slightly at the neck to show a collarless shirt with a white edge. He wore a black velvet beret-like hat. His portly gait carried with it an air of self-importance. He sat facing the congregation on a chair and once there was complete silence he stood up.

'I have been asked to speak to you today by Herr von Kram, the Bürgermeister of Schmalkalden Town Council, which has responsibility for your jurisdiction.'

There was a quiet crescendo of whispering as the people turned to each other to ask what 'jurisdiction' meant.

'I think it means "hillside",' said one.

'No,' said another. 'It means we have to pay taxes to Schmalkalden Town Council.'

'Whatever it does mean, it probably isn't good news,' said someone else.

'Quiet!' One of the councillors turned with a disapproving gaze towards the people.

They bowed their heads deferentially, knowing the guards were watching.

The Sisters sat motionless, fearful of showing any discontent about the savagery that had led up to this moment. Sister Margarete held a pebble in her hand to remind her of Brother Wilhem.

The preacher cleared his throat.

'I am here to preach from Scripture – that is the inheritance we have received from Professor Martin Luther. Be warned, God will show his mighty wrath against those who interpret Scripture wrongly, such as those who stay fixed and blind, holding only on to the Old Covenant. Do not fall into temptation like them. God's salvation is by grace alone – the Scriptures say so without equivocation.'

Now there was another murmuring as what 'equivocation' meant.

'We are here to listen, not to question,' said one man to those behind him. Herr von Kram listened while imagining he was sitting in Philip of Hesse's castle telling him how he had brought the common people under the Protestant wing.

The preacher resumed after signalling his annoyance at yet another disruption.

'Hear what St Paul has to say in his letter to the church at Ephesus:

> But God, who is rich in mercy, because of His great love with which He loved us, even when we were dead in trespasses, made us alive together with Christ (by grace you have been saved), and raised us up together, and made us sit together in the heavenly places in Christ Jesus, that in the ages to come He might show the exceeding riches of His grace in His kindness toward us in Christ Jesus. For by grace you have been saved through faith, and that not of yourselves; it is the gift of God, not of works, lest anyone should boast.[5]

Most of the people in the church apart from the councillors, Sisters and friars could not read, so they were used to the Scriptures being interpreted for them. To hear them in their own language was a new experience, for they were used to hearing Scripture in Latin. Gezel had not listened to a word the preacher had said, but when he read the letter from St Paul in German, she sat up with a start.

The preacher assumed a greater level of pomposity as he began to wave his arms around. He raised his already high-pitched voice.

'We do not need statues to pray to! God hears us – we do not have to earn salvation; our Lord has paid the price, you are free in him – you do not need the Mass as a sacrifice. Our Lord Jesus was the one and final sacrifice. The Lord's Supper is a reminder of that complete sacrifice . . .'

---

5. Ephesians 2:4-9, NKJV.

Before he could continue, Ditmar stood up with rage in his gaunt face, his eyes blazing with fury.

'So why was Brother Wilhem sacrificed, then? And why was the bread and the wine desecrated by your soldiers in this very place?'

His fellow friar put his hand on Ditmar's arm. 'Ditmar – we need justice, but not at the expense of more violence!'

'Yes, Malcolm, but should we allow murder and the blasphemy of the Lord's Supper to go by, like a change in the weather?'

'That is not in our gift – it is for the Lord to decide,' Malcolm said gently, but loud enough for some of the congregation to hear.

The preacher looked at Herr von Kram, who immediately stood up. He glanced at his guards, and motioned towards the back of the church. As they moved towards Ditmar, he sat down. One of the soldiers went up and whispered something to him. Ditmar kept his head pointing downwards.

The preacher made an elaborate movement, showing his distaste for the interruption, and continued to explain how the bread and wine were the 'real' body and blood of Christ, but not the 'actual' body and blood of Christ – nobody understood what the preacher meant, but all the common people nodded dutifully. The Sisters remained quiet and Ditmar shook his head and scratched his nose. He had obviously persuaded himself that it was better to do that than speak out again, for without doubt, he would be arrested and thrown into prison.

Now the preacher smiled to himself and launched into an attack against the old order.

'For too long the common people have been held hostage by papal ordinances. How could the Lord God Almighty send another messenger when he has already sent his Son? And not just that – in 1397 the cardinals elected their second Pope. How could that be God speaking to us? For too long the Church has venerated Christian men and women and made them into little less than angels; and the mother of Jesus who died a mortal death – why is she held up as equal to our Lord? Did she die on the cross and rise again?'

Sister Mary did not change her expression while the preacher continued on; he seemed unusually practised in his words. She prayed quietly to herself: 'O Lord God, Holy Mother and our Saviour Jesus Christ, have mercy on your forgotten people, and save us from more bloodshed, murder and hunger. Help us to see beyond our traditions and into the tabernacle where your holiness dwells. Have mercy on us all, I pray. I commend Brother Wilhem's soul into your eternal care and pray for peace in this village.'

As she came back into hearing the preacher's voice, she heard: 'God has appointed the authorities, and the local magistrates and the mayor are therefore divinely appointed elders . . .' He drew breath and finished his sentence: 'The Church and the council are jointly responsible for the administration of all legal matters.'

Herr von Kram immediately stood up; this was an interruption which the preacher could not stop.

'What are you saying? I did not agree to that!' Herr von Kram fumed.

He approached the preacher and asked him through clenched teeth what he thought he was doing. The preacher was nonplussed and mumbled something about God's kingdom being one kingdom, and made a hasty retreat. Herr von Kram turned to the congregation.

'You are answerable to Schmalkalden Town Council and to me as the Bürgermeister for all matters except matters of belief,' he said, loudly. 'For them, you are answerable to the Church here in Saxony, not the one in Rome.'

Herr von Kram walked into the grounds and began to talk heatedly with one of the town councillors. The guards followed and the villagers began to talk.

Ditmar spotted the opportunity and found his voice again. He went to the entrance and shouted out: 'What about Brother Wilhem's murderer – when will he be brought to justice?'

The service had come to an unexpected end, and Herr von Kram's guards were unable to take any direct orders from him as he was now remonstrating with Herr Herland Schulz, the Lord of the Manor. Inside the abbey, the hum of talking drowned out the angry words from outside, and the Sisters began to sweep the floor clean – it was muddy from the villagers' boots.

Gezel sat in her pew as people got up to leave, and Sister Margarete could not avert her eyes. Fixed on each other, they just held their gaze. Then Sister Margarete started to shuffle away, but Gezel easily caught her up.

'Have you anything to tell me?' asked Gezel, trying her best to sound as if she did not care.

Sister Margarete's face lifted from its dark furrows. Gezel expected a rebuff, but instead she heard, 'I do, but not now. You should come back tomorrow and I will tell you what happened. Do you want to know?'

Gezel nodded and Sister Margarete said, 'Ten o'clock tomorrow,' and hobbled away.

The next morning, Gezel was there, sitting on a stone bench, and Sister Margarete began her story.

'My father could not pay his rent to the Church after his harvest failed and ten of his sheep died. He agreed to loan a third of his land to Bertelt, his brother, for one year in return for thirty groschen. The money was paid and my father paid his rent, but Bertelt would not return all of the land because he claimed my father had moved a boundary fence to his advantage. There was bad blood between them.

'The following year, my father did not have enough money for the rent again and after visiting the monastery I was told to go there – when I asked my father why, he simply said it was the only way we could pay our rent. I went to the monastery, where I met Brother Wilhem. I did what I had to do, and my family were allowed to stay on our land.

'When you were born after the best part of a year, my father said he could not afford to look after you and it would be a disgrace for the whole family. He went back to see the abbot, who arranged for you to be looked after by my older sister, Gude, and her husband, Albert, who were tenants of the local Lord of the Manor. He also arranged for me to join the abbey here. I did not see Brother Wilhem for a few years, but I heard that he sent food and clothing for you to Albert and Gude.

'When he started to come here to take Mass, he could not afford to reveal what had happened in the past as he feared that the Sisters might turn against me. I knew in my heart that he regretted his actions; he once said that he still spent many hours a week in silent penitence, as I still do.'

Gezel listened, her face motionless, her body turned in and her head almost sideways to Sister Margarete. Then she slowly looked up.

'So, I have followed in your footsteps: I do not remember receiving any food or clothing. I was made to work day and night; they treated me like a dog – even worse than a dog...'

She got up suddenly, and left. How could she say anything more? Gezel felt too hurt to see beyond her own wretched life. As she walked back home, her thoughts collided into one another: 'You expect me to be sorry for you! You must have known where I was... Gude and Albert stole my food parcels...they almost starved me!'

Sister Margarete sat for several more minutes and then a tear rolled down her cheek. It was time for private prayer in the church, except that Sister Margarete could no longer bear to go in there unless a service was taking place. She went back to her own room, but she could not find any words to pray.

Had her soul started to journey to purgatory already?

# 5

# Expediency

Herr von Kram was in the sitting room of his large house in Schmalkalden, waiting impatiently for Martin Bucer, a theologian famed for his political acumen. He sipped some schnapps and by the time Bucer appeared, he had drunk at least two or three small glasses. He preferred to pour it himself rather than let the servant talk to the other staff about how much he had drunk.

Martin Bucer came in and was introduced by the butler.

Herr von Kram said, 'Thank you!', which the butler knew was a signal for him to leave them in private. Herr von Kram was in no mood for niceties.

'Why did you send us a preacher who wants the Bürgermeister to call himself a church elder? Are we to be made to look like fools in front of the common people? They will be confused as to who they should obey. What have you to say?'

'I assure you, Herr von Kram, I will not send him to you again. Since his visit to you, I have since discovered that he has been influenced by the teachings of Zwingli; a man who says those in authority should hold a Bible in one hand and a sword in the other – Church and State in his mind should be a single authority. I apologise – sometimes theological enthusiasm can get the better of us. Professors Luther and Melanchthon have taught us that we can be saved without the Pope or the saints – their followers sometimes try to emulate their boldness without their understanding.'

Herr von Kram listened without changing his expression; he was not placated.

'If only it were just a question of words, but it is not; some people are now claiming that we permit murder. Brother Wilhem was killed by Schmalkaldic League soldiers and a Franciscan friar is publicly claiming that we accept such killing as part of our religion. Philip, Landgrave of Hesse, says he only asked his soldiers to make sure the abbeys and monasteries were aware of their presence as they walked through the countryside on their way to the garrison. He did not want to provoke a conflict, just offer a warning. And now his reputation is tarnished by marrying again when he is already married. John, the Elector of Saxony, is deeply distressed that Philip, his chief ally, is disgracing himself. He claims that Luther himself gave counsel in the matter and that you were also involved. What is going on?'

Bucer drew his breath and said, 'It was complicated; Melanchthon, Luther and I wrote a letter to the landgrave, who had suggested that it might be advisable to marry rather than satisfy his carnal appetites or divorce his first wife. Indeed, Pope Clement VII had previously suggested to Henry VIII of England that bigamy would be a preferable option to divorce. Professors Luther and Melanchthon both knew that the patriarchs, Abraham, Jacob and David had more than one wife. They concluded that bigamy could be allowed in exceptional circumstances. Luther encouraged Philip to reconsider but should he, in good conscience, consider it better to marry than to live a life of constant fornication, then he should marry a second wife, provided he kept it a secret. Were it to leak out to the common people, then they would copy the practice and see it as divine law, which it is not. That was Luther's advice.'

Bucer drew breath and continued: 'I only agreed, albeit reluctantly, because there was a chance that Philip would change his allegiance to the emperor and by default then support the papacy. The reason he has tried to bring Rome and Saxony together as far as doctrine is concerned is, in my opinion, more political than theological. I suspect he sees theology as a set of rules to get round rather than live by. Without the permission of John Frederick, Elector of Saxony, Duke Maurice of Saxony and that of theologians such as Melanchthon and Luther, Margarethe von der Saale's mother would not have given her consent to the marriage. Melanchthon and I were present at the ceremony, although we had no prior knowledge of what we were being invited to; it was all we could do to prevent one of our main protectors defecting and leaving us vulnerable to Charles V's resurgence. The issue in itself is of no consequence to the papal tradition. In 1521 the Pope granted retrospective permission to Henry IV of Castile, who died in 1474, to marry a second wife as his first wife was childless. The judgement was that if his second wife bore him no children within a period of time, he was to return to the first wife. Bigamy was permitted by the highest authority in the Catholic Church. What matters now is that if we completely oppose Philip's request, he might become even friendlier with Charles V than he already is.'

Herr von Kram raised his eyebrows. That was all very interesting, but for him the main issue was one of public order. He had already concluded that only a trial of an alleged murderer would keep the people in the surrounding villages from taking the law into their own hands. He sipped his drink.

'There must be a trial,' he said without looking at Bucer, 'and the common people must know that the law cannot be taken into their own hands, whatever the result of the trial.'

'You are correct,' Bucer replied in a deferential tone. 'No one was more serious about the use of force to put down the peasants' revolt in 1524 than Luther. For him, theological truth could never be used to disobey the authorities which God himself has put in place to keep good order.'

Herr von Kram called for his secretary. An obsequious, slightly hunched man with paper and a quill entered the room. His whole body exuded deference to his master. Her von Kram was in no mood to equivocate.

'Find out who the man the people are saying killed Brother Wilhem is, and draft a letter to Philip, Landgrave of Hesse, to say this man must be arrested and tried for the sake of public order, and it must be done by the spring while it is still in the minds of the villagers. Then contact a magistrate and apply for an order of arrest.'

As the secretary left the room, he called out after him, 'Yes, and also contact an executioner, in case we need to use his services.' He turned to Bucer. 'Thank you for your visit, Herr Bucer,' he said without emotion. 'Can I rely on you to find a preacher who confines himself to teaching theology, and does not spill over into trying to commandeer public opinion as to who should exercise authority over the common people?'

'Of course, Bürgermeister; there will be no confusion from here on, I assure you. Thank you for your time.' With that, Bucer rose and left, glancing at the schnapps which had not been offered to him.

Soon a letter arrived for Herr Von Kram. It had the seal of Philip, Landgrave of Hesse, on it. The secretary, hunched and grovelling, brought it in.

'Read it,' said Von Kram, 'but get me some more schnapps first. And hurry!'

The secretary rushed out and barked an order to one of the servants. His voice had an almost screeching desperation about it. He came back into the room, composed himself and broke the seal of the letter. The servant scuffed in with a new decanter of schnapps and scampered out, apparently sensing that proceedings could not begin with her there.

The secretary started to read.

Dear Bürgermeister Von Kram

Thank you for your letter regarding the public order issue and the allegation that a member of the Schmalkaldic League murdered a priest, Brother Wilhem, recently, when he was taking Mass at the abbey at Rotterode.

I am mindful of any public disorder and remember the peasants' revolt in 1524 which had to be stamped on in order to prevent an outbreak of lawlessness. I specifically gave my soldiers instructions to warn but not provoke any kind of uprising. Whether or not the alleged has committed a murder is entirely another matter, and should be subject to a trial.

I will arrange for a magistrate to oversee the proceedings when the weather will allow the common people to attend and enjoy the event at the village of Fambach on Saturday 15 March. I will attend the proceedings.

Whereas there is a need for the common people to know that they cannot take the law into their own hands, there is equally a pressing case to be ready should the Holy Roman Emperor, Charles V, turn his attentions away from his campaigns in France and Turkey and focus on the German principalities. It is my judgement that we may not have the power to overturn his entire army, should they ever congregate in one place, but that we may be able to reach an agreement with him not to compromise the sovereignty and religion of the German principalities. It is, therefore, necessary to reach a judgement in this case which is both instrumental in maintaining public order as well as ensuring that the soldiers of the Schmalkaldic League are not demoralised to the point of defection. I will therefore be liaising with the magistrate to ensure that a proper balance is reached.

I am also aware that disputes about theological matters and rivalries between Maurice, Duke of Saxony and John Frederick of Saxony could also weaken our position in relation to the Holy Roman Emperor, and I would ask for your interventions to stave off such possibilities if at all possible.

However, in relation to the trial, please ensure that as many of the local people are made aware of the forthcoming trial, including any potential rebels who might imagine there is an opportunity to take advantage of the situation.

Sealed

Landgrave Philip of Hesse

Herr Von Kram looked at his secretary, who instantly took out some paper and sat at a table in the corner of the room. Her von Kram did not like to repeat himself.

'Make sure the common people know of the trial, and make sure that you find something else to whet the common people's appetite to begin with. Arrange for a market to take place on the village green at Fambach on the day, and have the executioner arrive two days before to erect the platform. Make sure it is strong enough for an executioner's block, should we need one for any who are guilty of a crime deserving of death or for those who see fit to rebel against the decision of the court. Give the villagers a tankard of ale each, and make sure there is plenty of food.'

The secretary walked backwards to the door and closed it gently behind him. Herr Von Kram poured himself one more glass of schnapps; he wondered if his supply of it would soon dry up. He relied on the Jewish traders in Hesse and Saxony for his supply of schnapps and other luxuries, but they were now under threat because of their failure to convert to Lutheranism. Such was the feeling against them that even if they were forced to convert, they might still be stopped from trading.

He shook his head, drank up and poured himself another.

# 6

# The Trial – the Medieval Way

The tables and long benches had been set out two days before. Hot coal fires for the hog roasting were lit as the sun rose. After an hour, when the redness of the coal had overtaken its deadened blackness, the hogs were hoisted up on spits, each resting on two tripods. The smell of meat slowly filtered into the air, and by the middle of the morning, the crackling from the fire added to the anticipation of the feast. The hog would be served with spelt bread, gruel and ale for the peasants. The local dignitaries would be served with the more delicate wheaten bread with butter; the best of the hog along with rich red wine would also be kept for the better-off. Apples, pears and strawberries would be available for all. A large number of wooden plates, copper jugs, bowls and wooden spoons were brought over from the Manor House. A horse-drawn cart arrived with many barrels of ale, and burly draymen began to unload them.

The servants began to scurry around and the village green came to life; the whispers of a quiet breeze blowing across it quickened into an ever-increasing bustle of feast-building sounds. Tinkers, jugglers and beggars seemed to emerge from different directions; Landgrave Philip and Bürgermeister Von Kram had made sure that enough of their soldiers and officials were in place to keep good order. The peasants, the butchers, the cobblers, the tanners and the sack carriers all came, hoping to watch the trial and find a seat at the tables to sample the roast hog, drinking as much ale as they could. Some of the better-off peasants had buttons sewn onto their lapels, and one or two wore blue trousers, which came out for festive occasions; anything too ornate for a peasant to wear could be spotted by the council officials and potentially confiscated. For once, children played happily with each other without being scolded.

The bankers, council officials, local nobility and jurors naturally separated themselves from the lower echelons. Their more colourful clothes, longer hair and the women's narrow belts decorated with copper plating were enough to signal where they sat in the social hierarchy. They also had prime position near the pond, where the executioner had built a solid platform using four empty barrels to give it the height necessary for public viewing. On this platform he could either behead an offender on a heavy block, or tie them up in a sack and throw them into the pond, and then hold them underwater with a long pole. The option of live burial would have taken longer than two days to prepare for, although many had come hoping to see just that. The vicarious horror was, for the spectators, a temporary release from the grinding misery of their lives.

When Landgrave Philip and Bürgermeister Von Kram arrived, there was an immediate quietening from the growing throng. They were ushered to a cordoned-off area near the pond. There Herr Von Kram was introduced to Philip's secretary, who would organise the trial proceedings. For half an hour intense discussion took place, and some anxious looks were cast along the main road which led into the village green. Eventually two carts with cages arrived; in one of them was a ragged middle-aged woman who was tied to a chair. Claus, the *landsknecht*, was in the second cage, smiling.

Philip's secretary gave orders for the local jurors to assemble and the crowd stood around the makeshift court. A roughly made dock was carried onto the grass adjacent to a grand chair, where the visiting magistrate, Herr Altmann, would sit. Herr Von Kram stared unemotionally, despite his prime concern that the crowd should be under no illusion as to where the authority lay.

The ragged woman was untied from her chair and led out of the cage. She came into view and was pushed into a kneeling position at the side of the dock.

'What is the complaint?' Herr Altmann barked.

One of Von Kram's officers stood up, announcing the charge: 'It is said this woman has the mark of a witch on her arm – she feels no pain when it is pierced.'

The magistrate's expression of disdain was displayed for all to see as he gave his order: 'Let us see what the thumb screws do . . . Executioner!'

The executioner beckoned the officers to bring the woman up onto the platform. She was tied to a chair facing the crowd, who by now had fully sampled the ale. The thumb screws were placed onto each of her hands and gradually tightened by the executioner. He remained impassive as the woman began to scream.

'What do you want?' she cried. 'You will kill me anyway!'

In a matter-of-fact voice, the executioner replied, 'You must confess to being a witch and then you will be treated with mercy.'

'You will drown me rather than bury me alive – is that mercy?' The woman laughed and spat, 'I am a widow and I pray to the moon, for there is no one else to pray to, but that is all; I am not a witch!'

The crowd began to chant, 'Witch, witch, witch!'

The magistrate stood and called for order, raising his arms. 'Tighten the thumbscrews and let us see if she will speak the truth then.'

The woman began to twist her body in agony and after several deep and prolonged moans, she spoke in a broken voice.

'Stop, please stop; if you want me to say I am a sorcerer, then I am – take me to my eternal home.'

The magistrate sighed and looked directly at Philip Landgrave and Bürgermeister Von Kram. He asked the jurors if she was guilty; they all nodded and he spoke out his judgement.

'This court will show mercy; she will not be subject to excessive punishment before her final fate. She has confessed quickly to the despicable and satanic practice of witchcraft. She is the cause of our poor harvests over the last three years. Praying to the moon, which the devil hides behind, has brought drought over our land. Let her be tied up in a sack and drowned before our very eyes. Professor Luther confirms that the executioner's hand is the hand of God. Go ahead and do the Lord's bidding.'

Out of the drunken crowd stepped Brother Malcolm.

Brother Ditmar tried to restrain him. 'There is no need,' he said, trying to tug at Brother Malcolm's robe.

Brother Malcolm was determined and firmly took brother Ditmar's arm off the robe. He strode forward and addressed the magistrate. His voice had no fear in it.

'Your honour, you have made your judgement. May I with your gracious permission say some final prayers with the condemned woman? I believe that God loves every single person on this earth, regardless of what they have or have not done. Please grant me this request. Please remember that our Lord spoke with outcasts when he taught and healed them. I await your decision.'

The magistrate looked over to Bürgermeister Von Kram, who in turn looked at Philip, who waited for a few seconds. He then nodded to Von Kram, who in turn gave his assent to the magistrate simply through a look in his eyes. The executioner beckoned Malcolm onto the platform and removed the thumbscrews, which had been loosened after her 'confession'. Malcolm ignored the crowd's derisory comments – but afterwards he remembered every one of them, and would privately struggle, wishing he could forget their jibes:

'Why don't you let her cast one more spell?'

'If you care that much about her, get in the sack and swim to hell with her – she could do with some company on the way!'

'Careful you don't touch the witch's mark on her arm or you'll end up in the river with her!'

Malcolm knelt down beside her, asked for her name and began to pray: 'Father God, your thoughts are higher than ours; we thank you that your mercy stems from your absolute holiness and righteousness. As you, Lord Jesus, were tried and sent to your earthly death when you had done no wrong, so we ask that you would comfort this woman in her plight, and bless her as she travels from this home to her eternal rest.'

When the landgrave's secretary heard Malcolm pray, his face screwed itself into a look of angry disdain; he also knew that to kill another priest could attract unwanted attention from those who supported the Holy Roman Emperor. He was incensed and about to intervene when Malcolm looked him in the eye, rose up and walked away.

Ditmar came to Malcolm and grabbed his arm.

'What are you doing, in the name of heaven? We have come to see if Brother Wilhem's murderer will be dealt with justly, even though there is little chance of that – we do not want to be removed from the crowd before the trial even starts!'

Malcolm was used to Ditmar's hot-headedness, and he smiled a little. 'We are here to minister to the beggars and the misfits, just as our Lord did. Do not worry; God will walk with us.'

Now the drunken crowd would see the ghastly spectacle unfold before them as the executioner whispered something in the woman's ear. She stood up and stepped into the bag, crossing herself. A rope was used to tie the top of the bag closed. Two of Bürgermeister Von Kram's soldiers carried the bag, wading into the middle of the pond. The men used two poles to hold the bag underwater. There was hardly any movement from the stricken woman and after ten minutes her limp corpse was hauled out and put on display at the edge of the pond. One of the poles was driven into the earth and she was tied to it underneath her arms, her head flopping to one side. Some of the children ran up close to her, but shouts from their inebriated parents not to touch her drew them back.

# 7

# The Trial Continues– the New Way

Claus was laughing from inside the cage as one of the soldiers opened the door and handed him a tankard of ale and a shank of roasted hog. He looked completely at ease as some of the villagers crowded around.

'Are you a murderer?' one of the villagers called out.

'Leave it to the judge, or I might murder you when I am released!' Claus bellowed.

The guards laughed out of fear, and even though the villagers had eaten and drunk more than they would normally do in a month, they thought twice before baiting Claus any further. He was Philip Landgrave's soldier and they knew that village justice was like a twisting and darting snake; it could spring back onto you in an instant without warning.

Some of the jurors were tenants of Herr Von Kram, some were from the local nobility and four others were hand-picked by Philip Landgrave. The magistrate, Herr Altmann, drew himself up in a gesture of self-importance and addressed the jurors.

'You are called to the honourable place of a juror in this trial. Please be aware that the case we are about to hear is far more significant than the drowning of a witch or the hanging of a thief. The soldiers of the Schmalkaldic League are the servants of God's appointed rulers, Philip, Landgrave of Hesse and Frederick, Elector of Saxony. We are here to show the common people that they cannot take the law into their own hands, but also that soldiers employed by our rulers deserve protection from the law as they preserve the religion and the way of life we treasure. I order you to keep these principles in mind as you follow the proceedings which I will lead.'

The jurors, who had previously been enjoying the feast knew their privileged position depended on their compliance. Herr Altmann sat down in his chair. A few others had joined the throng. Brothers Ditmar and Malcolm were among them. At the back there were a few of the Sisters; Sister Margarete could not travel but she had asked Sister Mary to tell her the outcome, even though she was already convinced as to what would happen.

Claus was escorted into the makeshift dock by two soldiers. The executioner was wearing his uniform, a long-sleeved top and two circular frills from the waist down; his tight-fitting leggings and leather shoes gave him the flexibility to carry out his duties. He waited on the platform, sitting impassively next to a beheading block and axe leaning up against it. As he was escorted to his place, Claus caught Gezel's eye and he winked. She looked back at him, expressionless.

Herr Altmann explained to the court that Bürgermeister Von Kram had received a letter from Father Hermann from the monastery at Bermbach explaining that Brother Wilhem was simply carrying out his duty to God when he was cut down. He told the jurors and the crowd that an allegation of murder had been made against Claus Brendell, a soldier in the Schmalkaldic League. A sudden hush came over the crowd as Herr Altmann called Philip, Landgrave of Hesse, to speak to the jurors. He bowed his head as he invited Philip to speak.

'Please, our respected Landgrave of Hesse, can you inform the court what the orders were given to the League who visited the abbey where Brother Wilhem died?'

Philip walked on to the executioner's platform, where he could be seen by everyone.

'The Schmalkaldic League is a defensive league set up to ensure that the reformed Church, which saw its beginnings in the teachings of Professor Luther, is not beaten back by the priestly intentions of the Pope Paul III, supported by the Holy Roman Emperor, Charles V. Individual strategic decisions are the responsibility of the individual regiments involved in any particular action.'

With that, Philip stood down and Herr Altmann asked the officer in charge to step forward. No one came forward and after a few seconds, Claus spoke from the dock: 'I was the officer in charge, your honour. We were on our way to the barracks when we came across the abbey and discovered that a Mass was being conducted in a flagrant disregard of our leader's expectations of the way the people should conduct themselves in worship. I did feel angry on behalf of His Excellency Philip, Landgrave of Hesse, and I admit I encouraged our men to bring down the idols which represent the evils of papal rule.

'Brother Wilhem tried to physically prevent us from carrying out our duties, shouting, "Stop, stop! These are the statues of our precious Holy Mother and our saints. You cannot do this or you will suffer the fires of hell."

'As the crowd of soldiers gathered round him, he began to stuff the bread and wine down his own throat and threw himself onto my spear. I never set out to kill this priest or any other, especially in a place of worship. We left soon after and continued on our journey to the barracks.'

Herr Altmann asked if there were any other witnesses and one of the soldiers, Stephan, stepped forward: 'I saw Brother Wilhem run towards Claus and he was completely out of control, stuffing the bread and wine down himself in case it should be defiled by a soldier's hands. He was not going to stand there and do nothing. He definitely ran himself onto Claus' spear. I am almost certain Claus returned to the barracks with his spear. Some of the other soldiers carried spears but they were not near the priest. I do not believe Claus is guilty of the charge; he was simply doing his duty.'

As Stephan moved away, Sister Mary stepped forward. She spoke clearly and looked directly at Herr Altmann.

'The soldiers came into our church during Holy Mass and immediately started to destroy the statues. When Brother Wilhem objected, they crowded round him. It seemed as if he would have continued to reason with them but his words came to an abrupt halt and I heard a deep groaning; it was a man's voice. The other Sisters and I were terrified; I did not see what happened but I heard one of the soldiers say, "He deserved it; why don't we feed him with his own bread and wine?" The others said, "Yes, let's teach him a lesson, even if he won't remember it." The soldiers made a lot of noise and left the church laughing.'

The jurors and the crowd were taken aback by the boldness of Sister Mary's testimony. They still had an inbuilt sense of deference to the Church, but Sister Mary had a quiet, dignified authority of her own. Herr Altmann turned to the jurors as there were no further witnesses.

'There is no evidence to convict this loyal soldier of the accusation that Father Hermann has made in his letter to Philip, Landgrave of Hesse. This unfortunate incident appears to be the result of an overzealous priest trying to defend his own peculiar heresy. I recommend to the jurors that Claus Brendell be acquitted of the charge of murder and be allowed to continue with his military duties.'

The jurors nodded in full agreement, and looked over to Bürgermeister Von Kram and Philip, Landgrave of Hesse, in the hope that they would be recognised for their part in the outcome. Claus walked free.

Claus, Stephan and several other soldiers began to talk loudly. Claus's self-belief had not abated.

'Where is Gezel?' he demanded. 'I'm sure she will want to celebrate with me – I saw her in the crowd. She will be looking for me. Hey, Stephan, can you get me another jug of ale?'

One of the officers came over and asked Claus to go and see Philip, Landgrave of Hesse, and Bürgermeister Herr Von Kram. Claus felt very pleased with himself but his demeanour changed as he approached them. Philip spoke to him without any sense of gratitude.

'Do not repeat these kinds of killings, or you will be dismissed. You will have plenty to do if the Holy Roman Emperor's soldiers try to regain our principalities for Rome. Spare yourself and your men. That is all.'

Claus was taken aback but bowed in deference and went back to his men, who looked at him wanting to know what had been said.

'He just wanted to say thank you to us for all we have done,' he muttered, 'but we must not endanger the life of a priest again.'

The soldiers paused for a moment but then carried on with the feast.

The sun began to go down as the woman drowned as a witch was set alight. As the sodden body was engulfed in flames, Philip, Landgave of Hesse, turned his back on the scene and took the opportunity to speak to Herr Von Kram.

'We do not need hotheads like Claus. The emperor has already taken against me for marrying a second wife and my son-in-law, Maurice, has recently helped the emperor against the Turks. I think Maurice is planning to mount an attack on John Frederick of Saxony. If he battles against him, then it will weaken the Defence League and give the emperor an opportunity . . .' He paused for a moment: 'I do not know what lies ahead, but we are not as strong as we were. At least the soldiers now know not to take matters into their own hands.'

With that he turned and walked to his carriage. Herr Von Kram wondered what he would do should Philip change his allegiance back to the emperor and the Church of Rome. God had appointed him as ruler, so he was entitled to change his mind; that was the easy part. The difficulty would lie in knowing exactly when to switch his loyalties, along with Philip of Hesse, back to the Holy Roman Emperor. Too soon and he and his entourage might become isolated if Philip changed his mind. Too late and he might be classed as the 'enemy'.

Herr Von Kram turned and walked back to his carriage. Behind him the flames began to subside.

# PART 2

Unexpected Journeys

# 8

# Walking Back to the Abbey

Gezel left the village green immediately after the verdict on Claus was announced, making sure he did not see her. Sister Mary was a little way ahead of her with the other Sisters, but for the moment Gezel kept her distance. It was Sister Mary's voice at the trial that she kept on hearing, not even the exact words, but the way she said them. Her mind began to swirl. Was this the first time in her life she had heard a woman stand up in front of a baying crowd without a shred of fear? Gezel envied such courage. Her own life was no more than a queue of people who wanted to use her; Albert and Gude, Bertold and Hette and now men like Claus. How could she be anything but the prostitute she was? People like Sister Mary seemed so far away, but not just in her way of life – in herself – was it going too far to imagine stepping into it? Would it not be better to go back to the tavern and let Claus have his way with her that evening? That is what Hette would expect of her and, after all, Hette was the only woman who had ever shown her any shred of care.

Something else began to echo in Gezel's mind: What would her father have looked like now? Her feelings towards her mother had already begun to change; what choice did she have but to go and pleasure Wilhem so her parents could 'pay' their rent?

Gezel was the unintended consequence of that rent payment. Suddenly the thought of Claus paying Hette for one hour's 'work' made her recoil. The smirk on his face as he addressed the magistrate, but most of all, the wink he gave her as he strode into the dock made her angry. Because she was scared of hell, she wondered if she had a right to be angry. One message had been given to her since her very first hour on this earth – she was worthless.

Gezel walked on and then eventually caught up with Sister Mary, quietly asking her if she could go back to the abbey with them.

Sister Mary knew that Gezel had recently seen Sister Margarete at the abbey but had presumed it was about Gezel's life at the inn; perhaps it was about seeking a different life. she was completely unaware that Gezel was Sister Margarete's child. She looked at her gently and said, 'Of course, it's not far now.'

For ten minutes they walked side by side. Then Sister Mary asked, 'Did you want to say something more?'

Gezel shook her head and thought to herself how frightened she was of good people – they could never understand people like her. Perhaps her moment of courage was a passing glimpse of a life she could never have, and that evening she would most likely be back at the inn satisfying Claus and his friends.

Then suddenly she spoke.

'Can the sins of a whore ever be forgiven, or will that woman go into the eternal flames on the last day? Once a whore, are you lost forever?'

Sister Mary thought for a moment and asked her if she knew what Christ said to the Pharisees when they brought a woman caught in adultery to him because according to the Law she had to be stoned? Gezel shook her head.

'He said, "Let him who is without sin among you be the first to throw a stone".'[6]

Sister Mary stopped quite suddenly and picked up one of the stones on the path. Looking at it in the palm of her hand she caught Gezel's eye, and then let it drop. Gezel stood still for a few moments before they carried on.

---

6. John 8:7, ESV.

They went down past the small plots of tenant land that were no longer under the abbey's control; Herr Von Kram was now the landlord. Of the few tenants that had not gone to watch the trial, not a single one of them greeted the Sisters as they passed by. Two small children waved tentatively, carefully checking that their parents were not watching. Gezel sensed the unspoken bond between the Sisters as they walked on with their heads slightly bowed. She thought to herself, 'What kind of strength is this? They do not have weapons strapped to their sides. What must it feel to belong somewhere? What is it that keeps them so single-minded?'

As they left the tenant farms with their stony earth, fluttering chickens and ragged dogs, they were now by the side of a forested slope. Reaching the apex of the slope, the abbey came into view. It was a building that was no longer a place of safety from the prospect of purgatory, but a defenceless church open to attack from anyone; the change from the sacred to the unholy had transformed the abbey's image – it had become a symbol of a conflict between princes.

Sister Mary spoke to Gezel as they began to descend the slope.

'I think I need to ask you why you want to come with us. I have to tell our abbess why you have come.'

'I want to ask my mother to take me on as a servant,' Gezel answered.

Sister Mary paused. 'You mean your Holy Mother?'

'No. My real mother, Sister Margarete – she was made to lie with Brother Wilhem by her father as he could not pay his rent.'

Silence followed.

Gezel stopped, realising that the Sisters were stunned by her words, but a life of subservience meant that they would say nothing. She noticed a flicker of the eyes in one Sister but that was all. She drew breath: 'I was given to an aunt and my mother joined Holy Orders as her parents could not afford to keep me. I ran away from my aunt and ended up at the inn. I have become a working girl there. If Sister Margarete rejects me, I will have to go back or I will starve.'

'You must speak to her after we arrive,' said Sister Mary, at last.

The tension was palpable. Gezel tried to think of the conversations they might have out of her earshot later on; for their own sakes, she imagined they would hope that Sister Margarete would send Gezel on her way, for she could only make things worse for them. Was she putting her mother in another impossible dilemma? First, her birth and now her return from a life of sin.

The first thing that struck Gezel was how cold the abbey was. The stone cloisters, the dormitory and the church itself would never be warm even in the height of summer; the atmosphere was statuesque, a place where laughter was unknown and darkness a comfort. This was a world where the fear of the unseen, ironically, was the most visible 'object'.

Sister Mary told Gezel to wait in the cloisters while the Sisters prepared for devotion. Even after their journey they did not think of taking food, or even a drink of water. After half an hour, the Sisters reappeared and went into the abbey for Compline, the last service of the day. Sister Mary came to Gezel and told her that Sister Margarete was not feeling well and so could not speak with her now; she would see her in the morning. She told Gezel to go to the kitchen and eat some bread and gruel; she was to sleep at the end of the dormitory on a bed of straw, near the door. She had left a small wooden cross on the straw.

Gezel waited a while; she could hear prayers in Latin, silence and then more prayers. Was that Sister Margarete's voice? Was she really unwell? The sounds of one of the prayers were vaguely familiar but Gezel did not know why. She thought that she should leave the cloisters before the service ended as she did not want to let Sister Margarete see her before the morning.

As she lay on the matted straw, which scratched her calf muscles and lower arms, she began to rehearse in her head what she might say.

'I know I am a sinner and have lived a sinful life . . . I know I do not deserve to live, but I beg you to take me on as your servant . . . I have nothing in my favour – my life is of no worth – I am worthless and God hates me . . .'

She kept on repeating the same thing in her mind over and over again. She began to wonder what Claus and Hette and the girls at the tavern must be thinking; no one would be concerned, except perhaps Hette. In among of all these half-thoughts, she fell asleep. When the Sisters returned, she did not wake up.

Gezel's imaginary words to Sister Margaret returned as she woke. The other Sisters did not speak, but the sound of splashing water and floor sweeping was enough to wake her. Gezel was completely disorientated; it was dark. This was the time that she normally went to sleep after a night's work. She guessed it must be around three o'clock in the morning and she felt sure the Sisters would return to their beds, but they left the dormitory. Where had they gone? Gezel was not sure what she should do, so she got up and went to explore. Once again she could hear prayers being said and silences. Then after half an hour or so, the Sisters appeared; some went to the kitchen and others sat quietly in the cloisters. After what seemed an age, the Sisters went back into the church for another service. It was now seven o'clock in the morning. Gezel had no idea of what the religious life was all about.

Sister Mary found Gezel and told her that after the Prime service, they would have a simple breakfast and then Sister Margarete would see her. Gezel should wait for her in the cloisters.

When the service finished around half-past seven, Sister Margarete came hobbling along.

'Come, let us speak,' she said, and they slowly made their way to the abbess' quarters. This was near the boundary wall, a small stone house with a wooden roof. Just outside the wall were two enclosures, one for pigs and one for goats and chickens. There was a heavy wooden door, and inside there was one main room with a table, two chairs and a bed. Some books and papers were piled on the table. In the corner was a small tin bath, and a few clothes were in a wooden box with a makeshift lid. There was a door leading out into another small room.

Sister Margarete slowly lowered herself onto one of the chairs. Gezel was unsure if she should offer to help.

Then Sister Margarete began with the last thing Gezel thought she would say. 'You have every cause to be angry with me, for I had no thought of the life I was creating for you. In the sight of God, I have sinned.'

Gezel fell to her knees, saying nothing. She had not expected such candour. But after a long silence, the words came tumbling out.

'I have no right to condemn you. You did what you had to do for your father to be excused his rent. I ran away from the life I had, and I have become the lowest of the low. My body is sold to give men pleasure. In return I have a roof over my head and food to eat. I have no choice who I service – the innkeeper's wife decides who I should go with. I am the real sinner; being a street girl has been my life. So if you have no room for me here as your servant, I will return to the life I came from and never come here again. I know I am wretched in the sight of men and God. Sister Mary told me of the story of the woman caught in adultery and Christ saying to the people, that the one who had not sinned should throw the first stone – that gave me courage to come and ask for your mercy, but I know deep down that the eternal flames are waiting for me. So do with me as you choose for this short time before I have to meet my end, whatever it is.'

Gezel kept her head down and wondered to herself how she had managed to speak all those words out. Was she talking to her own mother or was she talking to God? Or was she talking to herself? Was Sister Margarete listening as the abbess or as her mother?

Gezel was convinced that God had already made up his mind about her eternal destiny. In spite of this, she wondered what the prayers the Sisters said in Latin actually meant, and she wondered if she could ever learn to read the story of the woman caught in adultery.

Everything was slower in this place – would her life ever slow down enough for her to find peace?

She glanced up and saw Sister Margarete leaning forward with her head in her hands. Gezel thought that her mother was absorbing what she had said about her immoral life. Gezel silently rose and decided to leave the room, forgetting completely what Sister Margarete had initially said to her. As she began to close the door behind her, thinking she would have no alternative but to make her way back to the tavern, she suddenly heard Sister Margarete sobbing. Then she heard her say something but could not make out exactly what it was, except for her name. She went back; Sister Margarete looked up and held out her hands. Gezel knelt in front of her mother, took her hands and saw her mother's eyes soften. Tears of relief flowed down Gezel's face.

Sister Margarete began to speak very quietly.

'When I first came here, the abbess, her name was Gredechin, knew why I had been sent – because I had you out of wedlock. She thought giving birth an even greater sin than lying with a man outside of wedlock. She set me a routine of penance to demonstrate to the Sisters how grave my sin was. I lived with the pigs for two days a week, sleeping in the pen just outside here. The abbess told me it was a cross I should willingly bear; she expected me to welcome it. I was also made to fast, eating nothing during those two days and taking one tin of water to last me. Sometimes I would knock it over by mistake and then have nothing to drink. I carried out my bodily functions with the pigs. When the two days were over, I would rejoin the other Sisters. After the first time I had been outside for two days, I collapsed at Matins in the early hours. Abbess Gredechin said it was because of how great a sinner I was – she sent me outside for another day. It was only when I could no longer stand and had a high fever that they brought me back in. We had six services a day and I was asked to stay and pray for fifteen minutes longer every service; she demanded more and more prayers of repentance – spoken out loud.'

'Oh ... so is that what I have to go through?' Gezel asked.

'No, no, no – I do not blame you,' Sister Margarete replied, instantly. 'I blame myself for what your life has become.'

Gezel looked at her mother, realising she did not knew her at all. She never asked questions of anyone but this conversation was not like any other she had ever had.

'I cannot take it all in; but how have you ended up as the abbess when you were made to live with the pigs when you came here?'

Her mother shook her head. 'It is time for the service called Tierce; we will carry on talking after.'

As soon as Tierce was over at half-past nine, Sister Margarete came to Gezel, who was waiting in the cloisters, and they returned to Sister Margarete's house.

Sister Margarete carried on as if there had been no interruption: 'What I could not understand is that Father Hermann, the abbot, would come from time to time to take a few of the Sisters to the monastery where your father had become a Brother. I was in no position to challenge anything but I did notice that Abbess Gredechin herself never went with them. All she would say was that "men have authority over us because Eve came from Adam's rib – we must do what they tell us".

'At first I thought they were just going to the monastery to carry out domestic duties and cook food for the winter, but then on one occasion one of the Sisters became very distressed on her return and I decided to find out what was troubling her. She told me one of the Brothers had forced himself on her and the other Sisters were also made to succumb – they were told they were doing their duty to God, for God had created men with passion. I wanted to ask the abbess why these Sisters were not made to do penance as I had been, but I could not summon up the courage. One young Sister, she was only sixteen years old, was often chosen to go. When after one visit she did not return we were told she had contracted a high fever and died at the monastery. The burial was carried out in their own cemetery.

'Father Hermann did not come here again but one day Brother Wilhem, your father, did and spoke to Abbess Gredechin. As he made his way out of the compound, I followed him and caught him up – I wanted to know why he had come as I thought it concerned me and, to be honest, I also wanted to see him. We sat down on a log in the forest and he told me the real story.

'The young Sister had found out that she was pregnant and been told by Father Hermann to make herself miscarry the child. She had become angry and been told that she had disobeyed God by challenging the abbott. She ran off and was found drowned in a nearby river. When Brother Wilhem found out, he knew the time had come to challenge Father Hermann. He told Father Hermann that if the practice of taking Sisters to the monastery did not stop then he would leave the order and join the Protestants, and tell them what was going on. He then said, "I did wrong by you and our daughter – I cannot put that right but I can stop the same thing happening to others." I knew he had tried to.

'From that day on, no one ever came to take the Sisters to the monastery. Brother Wilhem started to visit us once a week and take Mass. Abbess Gredechin found herself more and more isolated, as the Sisters blamed her for the suicide of the young Sister. She decided to move to another abbey and no one was sorry to see her go. Father Hermann consulted Brother Wilhem as to who her successor should be, for he was now wary of Brother Wilhem's fearlessness. Father Hermann then spoke with the bishop, who sent a message asking me to become the abbess. That is how it happened. I would give it all up to be able to tell a different story.'

Gezel sat there, overcome by it all. Whereas before her father had in her eyes simply been like all the other men she serviced at the tavern, now she began to feel a strange attachment to him. Just months before, his body had been there in the very same abbey she was now in. It would be the closest she would ever get to him.

'Thank you,' she eventually said. 'I was sure you would condemn me. If I stay, will the Sisters turn against you? I am a prostitute.'

Gezel knew that the new Protestants would not be slow to hear the story that Gezel had left the inn and come to the abbey. The chatter at the tavern would find its way back to the Church leaders and they might cause even more trouble for the Sisters at the abbey. What about the Sisters themselves? What would they think?

'I think I have made a mistake; if I come here as a servant, it will bring trouble on you and the Sisters – they will know I am your daughter and both of our sinful lives will be condemned. What punishment will they inflict on you?'

Sister Margarete smiled. Her years of submission in prayer seemed to echo in her words: 'Why should we be afraid anymore? Look what trials we have come through and look how God has brought us together through your courage. Let us trust God to keep walking with us. I do not know why, but I feel that God is not angry with me or you. Perhaps you are right – they will try to punish me or humiliate me, but I would rather that than push you back to the life you have left. Then I would have something even worse to do penance for. You must not leave on my account. We do not know how long we have together. Let each day take care of itself.' She sighed. 'I think I must rest a while now.'

Gezel left and went back to the cloisters. Later on, she went to help in the kitchens. As the days went by, she began to work in the vegetable gardens, and sometimes walked with the Sisters to look after the children while the tenant wives went out to work in the fields to look after the livestock. Forgotten connections with the villagers began to open up again.

The abbey was no longer under the control of the Roman Church but what was now the Lutheran Church, although the Sisters were allowed to continue living there. The same building had a different atmosphere; there were no icons and the windows were plain. One thing that had not changed was that people went to church not so much to discover their eternal destiny but to find out what their earthly masters required of them.

Another Sunday service approached.

# 9

# A Sermon on Marriage

The story of Gezel returning to the abbey where her mother, Sister Margarete, was the abbess, had found its way back to Bürgermeister Herr Von Kram. He cared little about moral or theological problems, but was much more interested in how the Church's preoccupations could be used to reinforce his political position as Bürgermeister of Schmalkalden Town Council. Herr Von Kram took his time and made sure that the next preacher was properly briefed. He sipped his schnapps and went over in his mind what he would say to his appointed pastor, a man called Herr Godke.

'I want the people to know that the Church of Rome's teaching on celibacy is a lie and that my Town Council is fully behind exposing the consequences of that teaching. So, a child out of wedlock, fathered by a priest, who becomes a prostitute has now returned to her own mother who is the abbess of the church we use on Sundays; that is the church you will give your sermon in. Do not name them, but make sure everyone knows who you are talking about. Make sure that you expose such behaviour as typical of what the papacy allows under its domain, and condemn it as an abomination similar to those condemned by the God of the Old Testament.'

When the day came, Herr Von Kram sat in the front row next to the local Lord of the Manor, Herr Herland Schulz. The local nobility carefully took their seats just behind them. The villagers, the tenant farmers and their families respectfully filed in. The Sisters all sat at the back with Sister Margarete and Gezel beside each other. The preacher, Herr Godke, stood up and walked slowly to the front of the church. Turning round to face the congregation, he waited for complete silence; finally his grimace relaxed into a sombre stare.

'Today I am addressing you about the holy institution of marriage, and I am using the text of a sermon given by Professor Luther just twenty or so years ago.' He paused so the congregation could absorb the provenance of his words: 'Our Lord God in heaven has created man and woman to be joined together in holy matrimony. I start with the words of our Lord and Saviour when the Pharisees questioned Him about divorce...'

Gezel's mind filled up with the echoes of Herr Godke's voice; some of the words flew past her, but his tone was unmistakable. A child born out of wedlock was an offence to God. It was also tantamount to blasphemy for such a child to be reunited with her mother, a Catholic nun who was an abbess. Herr Godke did not name Sister Margarete and Gezel; he did not need to, for everyone knew who he meant. Suddenly the preacher's voice came back into focus...

'Let me explain: when a husband is denied his marital rights, he may be then tempted to disobey God's law outside of his marriage, and so in denying him, his wife is subjecting him to temptation which she has the power to remove. God has created him to procreate. So,' he said, after drawing breath, 'after public warnings, the man may dispense with his wife and take another. There has been no marriage.

'Now, you may ask what the contrary case is, that is, where a husband is unable to fulfil his marital obligations. Professor Luther tells us that the wife then should seek the husband's permission to "secretly" be given to his brother while formally remaining his wife. The purpose of these rules is to maintain the order of creation – namely, that woman was created from the side of the man. Professor Luther even tells us how the wife should address her husband: 'Oh dear one, you cannot be a proper husband to me so in God's eyes we are not married – let me marry your brother in secrecy so you can still call yourself my husband and hold on to your property...'

Herr Von Kram and Herr Herland Schulz both nodded vigorously with obvious approval. Herr Godke continued on with a faint smile of self-satisfaction. His words once again faded, but with a jolt, Gezel suddenly woke up to what she felt was a thinly veiled attack on her parents: 'You may say without adequate means one cannot bring up children, for you have no food to give them. For this reason, parents might send their offspring into the priesthood, but Professor Luther tells us that this is purely a lack of faith. No excuse is beyond the grace of God; it is God's plan for nearly all that they marry and bring up children in the knowledge of salvation. Do you want to end up bringing harlots into this world? Professor Luther again gives us guidance: God will take care of feeding the children for after all he created the children; will He not feed His own children?'

Gezel began to register that her fate lay in the hands of a preacher who wanted to please the leader of the Town Council. Had it not been Herr Von Kram, it would have been someone else. Her mind was a blur, but she also heard something about God wanting the Jews to suffer because they had not converted to Christianity. The final words were spoken with authority: 'So before the congregation takes communion, let it be clear that any who take the wine and the bread are witnesses to the real presence of Christ in those sacraments. Do not parade your sins inside the tent of our Living God. It is better to stay in your place and seek God's mercy and change the direction of your heart to face him in his glory.'

The people filed to take the bread and the wine. The Sisters all stayed rooted to the spot with their heads held downwards. The villagers did not greet the Sisters as they left the church to return to their meagre Sunday lunches.

The Sisters took breakfast after the Prime service at 7 a.m.; it was taken in silent reflection. Conversations were allowed in the evenings after

Vespers at 5 p.m. when they came together to eat. Following Herr Godke's sermon the previous day, that particular meal was taken in almost complete silence. Gezel brought the food in and received the faintest of nods as she served the Sisters. She knew in her heart she could not stay at the abbey after what had been said in church. Herr Godke had given unspoken permission to the villagers to denigrate and humiliate the Sisters; the power of the preacher's self-assured moral certainty masked the true intention behind it. Simply being kind to the Sisters could be taken as a sign of disloyalty to Herr Von Kram and the local Lord of the Manor, Herr Herland Schulz. The villagers would be caught between what they wanted to do and what they had to do.

Gezel knew her continued presence as a child born out of wedlock and past life as a prostitute would magnify the risk to her mother and the other Sisters. The local tenants and their wives would no longer feel comfortable providing them with milk and bread in return for help with the children as they had begun to since the abbey started to be used for services. She planned to speak to her mother after the Compline service at 7 p.m. and tell her she had to leave as soon as she could. She had no specific plans; she just knew she had to go. To return to the tavern would not help the Sisters, for the story was out. She would have to disappear.

She approached her mother at the end of the meal and said she would need to speak to her after cleaning the kitchen. It was obvious to Gezel that Sister Margarete knew what was on her daughter's mind.

At half-past seven, Compline was over. The Sisters began to leave for private prayer in the cloisters when they heard a sudden rapid knocking on the abbey door. A man called Kaleb and his wife, Judith, were standing there with their ten-year-old daughter, Esther. Kaleb was beside himself while Judith was in obvious pain and discomfort, being heavily pregnant. Esther was crying. Behind them was a horse and cart laden with belongings. The Sisters gathered around, and Gezel came to see what the commotion was.

'Please help us,' Kaleb pleaded. 'We are cloth merchants living in Schmalkalden, but we have been forced to leave this evening. We have been paying the protection penny to the authorities and complying with their rules – we do not discuss our Jewish faith with anyone. Part of our trade is with the Turks, and to date they have allowed this. But this evening one of Martin Bucer's men came to our house demanding we convert immediately and that Esther be baptised straightaway. They accused us of siding with the God of Islam, shouting that we are helping them build up their armies – they use our cloth for their uniforms.

'Judith is unwell and about to give birth so I begged for time for her to have the child first before deciding if we could convert or be better off leaving for another country. One of the officials slapped me round the face and called me a heretic and a deceiver; they said they would be back in the morning. We panicked, knowing that they would not believe us whatever we said, even if we promised to follow their faith. Judith would not be able to cope with it all in her condition so I loaded up our horse and cart with as much as I could. We set off but Judith is in such pain we had to stop. We cannot continue on this evening. Please help us.'

Judith collapsed, falling to the floor. For a while she just whimpered but then began to scream. She said something in Yiddish, and Kaleb explained she was saying that her waters had broken. The Sisters had experience of helping some of the local women in labour, but after a few minutes it seemed that Judith was experiencing more severe problems. She was losing blood very quickly and it became clear that she would need the help of a doctor if she were to stand any chance at all.

Sister Margarete knew that in sending for a doctor the authorities would be alerted that they were harbouring a Jewish family. She saw the scene all those years ago when she herself had given birth to Gezel and a local doctor had come to her parents' small shack. While Sister Mary and two others were trying to help Judith as much as they could, the parable of the lost sheep came into Sister Margarete's mind; the shepherd left the ninety-nine sheep to look for the one who was lost.[7] She looked straight at Gezel: 'Go to Dr Arzt's and fetch him. We have to trust our God in heaven that Herr Von Kram will not punish us for taking this family in. He may do, but our lives are in peril whatever we do. May God help us and save this mother and baby. We are all in his hands.'

She looked at the Sisters' faces, a mixture of frowns, relief and fear, each one keeping their emotions at bay, as they always did.

Gezel knew where Dr Arzt's house was and ran straight there. After knocking loudly, a servant eventually came to the door. Gezel explained that a family had come to the abbey and that a woman in labour was in great distress, and asked if the doctor could come. The girl came back and said Dr Arzt wanted to know who the family were, and what their names were. Gezel said they were cloth merchants from Schmalkalden; the man was called Kaleb and the wife, Judith. They were on a journey – that was all she knew. The girl came back to the door and said Dr Arzt would not attend. Gezel asked why.

'Because they are Jewish,' said the servant, curtly, and closed the door.

One hour after leaving the abbey, Gezel arrived back. As she neared the door, she could hear wailing and sobbing. There on the floor was a shroud partially laid over the dead mother, with Esther holding on to her. Sister Mary was quietly washing the stone floor, and seemed

---

7. Matthew 18:12-13.

uncertain, as if she did not quite know if fully scrubbing the blood stains away would upset Esther even more.

Gezel went to Sister Margarete, who was sitting on a bench at the side of the church.

'The doctor will not come because they are Jewish,' she whispered.

Sister Margarete shook her head and muttered something. Gezel did not hear it but had made her mind up. 'I will go with them. It is not safe for them or for me to stay here, and it will be better for you and for all the Sisters. The soldiers will come in the morning if not before.'

Sister Margarete bowed her head and seemed to be praying. She paused and looked at Gezel with tears in her eyes. Gezel looked down as her own tears came. As she looked up, she saw Kaleb trying to stop himself shaking.

Kaleb already understood the imminent danger they were all in, but he would not leave without his wife and their stillborn child. It was against his tradition for her and the child not to have a Jewish burial.

'We will take them on the cart and find a rabbi along the way, but we cannot leave without them,' he spluttered.

'My daughter will come with you, for she also has to leave.'

Kaleb frowned.

'She will help you look after Esther,' Sister Margarete told him.

Kaleb's features relaxed and he nodded in gratitude, knowing he would need help if he was to drive the cart without stopping too often. He did not ask any questions, for he was in no position to refuse any help offered.

The Sisters tied up Judith's body in the shroud they had made from an old robe, and lifted it onto the cart; the blood began to darken patches of the whiteness. The tiny body of the baby was wrapped separately. Esther was given some shawls and Gezel put her arm around her as they sat with their legs over the side, next to Judith's body. Gezel hardly had a moment to say goodbye but had hugged her mother out of the sight of the other Sisters. She emerged with a small cloth bag which contained a Bible and a scarf; Sister Margarete had also given her a shawl and a small amount of money.

With an enormous effort, the horse pulled the cart into motion as the creaking and uneven jolting began. The silhouette in the moonlight slowly lumbered away from the abbey.

Esther accepted Gezel's quiet reassurance and after a few minutes rested her head on his shoulder. Without moving she said: 'Where are we going, Daddy?'

'We are going to Helmers, about eight miles from here, to see Uncle Jacob,' choked her father. 'He will know of a rabbi who can give our beloved Mummy and the baby a proper Jewish burial.'

'How long will it take and how will we dig the hole? It took those men all day when Aunty Sylvie died,' Esther said.

'About eight hours; we will find a way to dig the hole,' Kaleb replied, attempting a smile to comfort his daughter.

The horse was not in the prime of life and had gulped a great deal of water before they left. Kaleb had two sacks of hay and some apples to feed it, but in the desperate flight and tragic loss of Judith and the baby, more had been left behind than taken. Sister Mary walked for a mile or so beside them to make sure they were on the right track. In the darkness, the trees and wind could deceive so easily. Then she said her farewells, and turned back towards the abbey.

Esther put her hand out so she could touch her mother's face.

'Mummy's getting cold,' she said.

Gezel took the shawl her mother had given her and spread it over the shroud. Esther nodded. 'That's better; Mummy might feel better in the morning.'

Despite the constant uneven motion, Esther would not let her mother go, but after an hour she slowly subsided onto Gezel's lap. Gezel could see Kaleb's shoulders as he sat at the front holding the reins. He said nothing in the dark silence except for the occasional grunt of encouragement for the horse.

After two hours they stopped to give the horse a feed from a canvas bag. Kaleb looked at Gezel.

'The family I know in Helmers will know a rabbi. Judith and our child must have a proper burial. She must be carried away into the heavenly host in the Jewish way. You do not have to come to the burial if you do not wish to. You come from the Roman Church, don't you?'

Gezel nodded. 'I will come to the burial for Esther's sake, if you do not think I am intruding.'

'If Esther wants you to come, I would be grateful. Later, you can tell me why you cannot stay at the abbey – I do not know where we will travel to after. Perhaps Uncle Jacob will guide us as to where we should go.'

Kaleb took the bag away from the horse and climbed back up onto the cart. Esther was still fast asleep on Gezel's lap as the cart trundled off once more. The moonlight began to merge into the edge of the dawn light from behind the horizon. Gezel thought back to Kaleb's words: 'Uncle Jacob will guide us as to where we should go.'

# 10

# The Burial

They saw the shapes of the houses emerge as they reached the apex of a hill. Getting closer, they saw more movement; it looked as if some produce was being taken to the town square. Perhaps there was a market? Kaleb was reluctant to draw attention to the situation by going too far into the centre.

'You must stay here with Mummy, Esther. Gezel will look after you while I go and find Uncle Jacob – he will know of a rabbi. I will be back as soon as I can.'

Esther pined. 'Please bring something to eat, Daddy. Mummy will feel better soon and she will be hungry. And I want some *challah* bread too. Gezel is hungry, aren't you? What do you want?'

Kaleb held his daughter close. 'Mummy is going to sleep forever now. She isn't hungry. She loves you forever too. I will be back as soon as I can. We have to take Mummy and baby to a special place in a little while, and our tradition is that we will find a nice resting place in the ground for them to sleep forever.'

'Can I go to sleep with them?' Esther asked.

Kaleb shook his head. 'Mummy wants you to stay with me; you will get bored if you have to sleep forever. Just wait here and give the horse some apples.'

As Kaleb walked into the town, Esther asked Gezel what was in her bag. 'It's just a book my mother gave me when we left,' Gezel replied.

'What book?' Esther was curious.

'It's called the Bible,' Gezel replied.

'Let me see!' Esther leafed through Gezel's Vulgate Bible. Esther did not understand it, as it was in Latin. She looked at Gezel and said,

'Has it got the Ten Commandments in it? We have a book with them in called the Talmud. I will find it.'

Gezel nodded but she had to tell Esther that she couldn't read, so would not be able to find them.

Esther looked at Gezel in amazement. 'I will teach you the Ten Commandments in Yiddish,' she said. 'You can learn them before Daddy comes back and you can read them out loud. I am a good teacher; Mummy taught me. I want her to hear me teaching you before she goes to bed.'

Esther read through them and Gezel went along with it to keep her occupied. Although the script did not mean anything to Gezel, she thought she recognised some German-like sounds from the language. Esther realised that Gezel could not understand Yiddish so she read them out in German; translating from the Yiddish came naturally to her, as her mother had taught her both languages.

Esther went to the cart and found a piece of chalk from her belongings. She scraped away some loose earth and wrote onto the hard ground.

1. You shall have no other gods.
2. You shall not make idols.
3. You shall not misuse the name of the Lord.
4. Remember the Sabbath, keep it holy.
5. Honour your father and mother.

'Now you write them out,' she ordered Gezel. 'I am the teacher now.'

Gezel knelt down and copied the writing next to Esther's list. Esther looked over it with approval and then said, 'Now read them with me.' Gezel just pretended to read them while listening to Esther's phrases. Esther then wrote the whole alphabet down.

'Tell me,' she said, 'which letters are not in the first five commandments?'

Gezel spent a long time studying the shapes but then slowly copied these letters with the chalk 'c j k p q v x z'. They were beginning to run out of ground to write on.

'Good,' Esther said. 'You only missed one – the "w"; well done; I must go and check on Mummy just in case she's woken up.' She disappeared, and then came back. 'No, she's still asleep. Will we change her clothes before we put her in the ground? How long will Daddy be?'

Gezel reassured Esther as best she could. She began to get concerned as people went about their daily tasks; one or two carts of hay passed and two women carrying pails of milk looked curiously at them. About thirty minutes later, Kaleb came back with two young men, both with shovels.

'Where is Uncle Jacob?' Esther asked immediately.

'He is not well enough to travel,' Kaleb said, 'but he has given you this purple ribbon so you can wrap it round your finger. He says that when you touch the ribbon on your cheek it will bring Mummy's smile back.'

Esther wrapped it round her finger three times and Gezel helped her to tie it in a small, neat bow. She held it against her cheek but did not look at her mother's face.

Kaleb spoke quietly. 'These young men are Judah, Uncle Jacob's grandson, and Judah's cousin Samuel. Uncle Jacob says that Judah has a wish to be a rabbi and has studied the law. He will say the prayers. We will take Mummy and baby to a quiet place and they can rest in the ground together. Here, Esther, there is some bread and cold meat for you and you also, Gezel. We have milk, and some food for the horse. Take a few moments to eat and then we shall go.'

They stopped a mile and a half out of town. Samuel took them to a place about thirty metres into the trees. There was a gully, and the soil nearby was damp enough to dig.

'We need an hour to prepare the grave,' Judah said.

Esther immediately piped up, 'I want to see where Mummy is going to sleep. I can dig the hole in the ground too.'

'Yes, you can help,' Kaleb said, knowing that to upset Esther about anything at this moment would be unwise. 'Will you help, Gezel, please? But I will have to stay with the horse and cart to make sure it is not stolen.'

Gezel nodded and Esther held out her hand.

They returned to the road and were able to bring the horse and cart just inside the trees for cover. Judah and Samuel went back to start digging while Judith and the baby's bodies stayed on the cart. Esther and Gezel went with Judah and Samuel, but the work was too hard; they returned to the cart until the time came to carry the bodies to the graveside.

When the grave had been prepared, Judah and Samuel came back. Esther went round to the other side of the cart. She pulled out a dress from one of the bags.

'This is Mummy's favourite dress,' said a half-smiling Esther. 'Gezel will help me get her ready for bed.'

It was obvious to Gezel that Kaleb was immediately concerned as to how Esther would be when she saw the damage to her mother's body. Gezel raised her hand slightly to reassure him. The three men stepped a few paces away and turned their backs to Gezel and Esther. They put their skull caps on and Gezel could hear prayers being softly spoken in Yiddish.

Gezel told Esther to take the dress to put over Judith's head while she cut away the bloodstained parts of the robe around her midriff.

As she was about to remove the part of the sodden robe with a knife, she told Esther to look for a scarf in the bag. Esther left what she was doing and went to the bag but could not find a scarf. By the time she had finished looking, Gezel had put one of the shawls which the Sisters gave to Esther around Judith's waist.

'We have to find a scarf for Mummy's head,' Esther said anxiously.

'I have one,' Gezel replied, pulling out the small bag Sister Margarete had given her.

They took away the rest of the original robe and fitted the dress over Judith's head – Gezel took Judith's weight off the deck of the cart bit by bit and Esther slowly pulled it down. Esther then took the scarf and wrapped it carefully round her mother's neck.

'We're ready,' Esther called out and the three men turned and walked over.

At the grave, Judith and the baby were lowered in.

Judah began to pray and Esther piped up, 'Gezel cannot understand.'

'Judah will say the prayers in Yiddish and German afterwards,' said Kaleb, kindly.

Judah prayed: 'God, full of mercy, who dwells in the heights, provide a sure rest for Mummy and the baby upon your wings. May divine mercy protect them forever, and tie their souls with the rope of life. The everlasting is their heritage, and they shall rest peacefully upon their lying place, and let us say: Amen.'

He repeated the prayer in German. After more prayers, the time came to fill the grave. Esther began to push the soil in with her hands but then suddenly stopped: 'If Mummy and baby are going to sleep for a long time, how will they breathe?'

Kaleb picked up a long, thin dead twig and pushed it into the soft soil. 'The stick in the mud will have a very small gap round it and that will be enough for them both to breathe.'

Esther turned and took Gezel's hand and they walked back to the cart. Once they had gone, Kaleb knelt down and quietly wept. Judah and Samuel put their arms around him.

Wiping his face as dry as he could, he rose. 'Come, I must not let Esther see me too distressed.'

'Why have you been crying Daddy?' Esther asked when they got back to the cart.

'I am a bit sad because I will miss Mummy and baby, even though they are resting in the forest, God's resting place.'

Esther looked at her father carefully and led Gezel a few paces away from him. She whispered, 'I know Mummy and baby are dead. I think Daddy will not be so sad if we all say they are asleep.'

She clasped Gezel's hand as tightly as she could.

# 11

# Seeking Refuge

They returned to Uncle Jacob's house, where the sounds of quiet prayers and the smell of food somehow merged together. Uncle Jacob's wife had died several years before, and Judah's parents had left for Venice a few months earlier so they could make a living as money lenders in the Jewish quarter, as the port was a focal point for many traders in the Mediterranean world. Judah had stayed behind to care for his grandfather, and Samuel lived with his parents nearby. A local washerwoman came to the house each day to carry out domestic tasks and prepare food. She was the widow of a Jewish shoemaker, but was now only allowed menial work by the authorities.

The *kosher* lamb, bread and olives were bittersweet; food flavoured with sadness, fear and uncertainty. Kaleb was not hungry, but he still filled his plate up. They sat and ate in almost complete silence but for the clatter of plates. He waited till the meal was over before going to Uncle Jacob, on the other side of the room. They spoke in Yiddish, which Gezel could not understand. She sat cross-legged in the corner while Esther quietly went over the letters of the alphabet with her. Her father was saying something about getting to Amsterdam to make sure his wool was not stolen – she understood Yiddish and was used to him talking about his business.

Uncle Jacob explained to Kaleb that he and Esther could stay; the Town Council were willing to accept Jews on certain conditions. These were the payment of the 'extra penny' in tax, an undertaking not to act as money lenders and the promise not to promote their beliefs or discuss their religion with non-Jews. There was a slight apprehension in Uncle Jacob's voice which made Kaleb wonder if he had meant what he said. In any case, these were exactly the same rules the family had been living under in Schmalkalden before they were hounded out.

Uncle Jacob spoke with many hand gestures, and listening to him was like hearing the wind blow, sometimes quiet and other times furious: 'I am sorry, but that young woman cannot stay here with you and Esther!' he said. And then he began his lecture on the political situation. It appeared their ruler may turn Lutheran soon, and they were against the Jews because they had not converted. Someone called Josel von Rosheim had fought their corner but he was now discredited, and Luther had written a stinging condemnation of the Jews. The Ottoman Navy had not long captured 7,000 slaves from the Bay of Naples, so now was not a good time to be selling cloth to them for soldiers' uniforms.

'Go to Poland where many Ashkenazim Jews have gone or the Balkans – your trading connections will be waiting for you there,' Uncle Jacob said.

Esther looked up for a moment.

Uncle Jacob carried on talking about something called Auslauf where minorities, Catholic or Protestant, could travel to another province to attend their church, or gather outside city walls rather than emigrate, but he said this was not an option for Jews, who had to keep themselves to themselves...

'Uncle Jacob, why don't you take a rest? You have had a long day,' Kaleb suggested.

Uncle Jacob nodded, and in a few minutes his words became intermittent and he started to snore.

Kaleb went outside and put his head in his hands. He felt inconsolable in his heart but knew he had to stay in control for Esther's sake. Kaleb urgently wanted to go to Amsterdam, where up until now his wool from England would be delivered and transported to Schmalkalden. Normally the wool, after being cleaned with hot alkaline water and stale urine, would be spun into yarn by the local women he employed. They would pull the wool fibres into thin strips using their fingers; making the first part of the thread by twisting the fibres with their fingers, they would then attach it to a downward-pointing spindle. Once the weight of the spindle took over the twisting, the length was let out bit by bit. The wool yarn would then be made into a loose cloth material on a basic loom before the next stage, a pounding making it more tightly woven. The cloth would be dyed before being taken to Constantinople, where it would be sold to local merchants who would have it made up into uniforms for military officers and their soldiers. They would use the local women there to embroider the uniforms. Kaleb had to get to Amsterdam as soon as he could, otherwise he might lose his sources of wool fibre, which would have to be redirected to wherever he set up his new life. Perhaps Uncle Jacob was right about Poland.

He reminded himself that Esther had just lost her mother and had attached herself to Gezel; perhaps it was a useful distraction for her? Who would look after Esther while he went to Amsterdam? Judah would be out most days, and Uncle Jacob was too frail. And Esther would feel lost – at least she could occupy herself teaching Gezel to read if they were together; he could tell that Esther liked Gezel. He found himself in a daze, praying and asking God for help. He could not grieve in solitude as he had done for his own parents.

Esther waited till Uncle Jacob had fallen asleep and Kaleb had gone outside before speaking to Gezel: 'Uncle Jacob wants you to go away and me to stay here while Daddy goes to Amsterdam; he has to go there to get them to send the wool somewhere else called Poland. I don't want you to go – I'll be lonely and anyway, you must learn to read properly. I will go and tell him that he must take us with him. I will tell him I don't want to stay here without you.'

Gezel smiled, wryly wondering, as she did every day, what her fate would be.

By the time Judah had returned home at seven in the evening, Kaleb had thanked Uncle Jacob for his kind offer but told him that the three of them would make their way the next day and find a place for Gezel and Esther to stay nearer to the Low Countries while he travelled on to Amsterdam. It would be better for Uncle Jacob, Judah and the washerwoman to carry on without any changes. They had already shown great kindness to them in the midst of tragedy.

Judah felt he wanted to do something to help them, even though he knew they would be safer if they all left. He was also worried that his uncle's trade in clothing for Ottoman soldiers would be used against them if they stayed. But he still wanted to help.

'I heard them talking in the fields about a friar called Malcolm who they call the "witch's friend" – they say he said prayers with her at the trial in front of the prince and the Bürgermeister before they drowned her; nobody challenges him because he is a man of the Church who has a sincere heart and a deep faith – he may be able to help you gain safe passage; that is the sort of thing he does. His monastery is only an hour north-west of here at Bernshausen. I can take you there to see him, if you want me to.'

Gezel spoke up: 'I saw him at the trial; he is a brave man. The soldier on trial killed my father but they let him off, as they always do with soldiers.'

Kaleb paused, raised his eyebrows and waited a few moments before looking at Judah.

'Thank you so much – will you go with Gezel and ask this Malcolm if he can help us?'

'Are you a Jew, Brother Malcolm?' Ditmar asked him.

Brother Malcolm just looked at him with his calm, gentle smile. But Ditmar would not let it be, and carried on, 'Why is the Lord's purpose served in taking Jews to safety? If the Protestants drive them out of our neighbourhood, they are saving us a task, aren't they?'

Malcolm replied, 'Have you not read the parable of the Good Samaritan?[8] Who is my neighbour?'

Ditmar sprang back, 'A dead Samaritan cannot help anyone; you could be kidnapped, especially if you are travelling with a Jew who looks as if he has money. How can you keep safe?'

Malcolm thought for a few seconds. 'If the Lord calls us to go, we have to trust him. If the apostles had returned to their homes, where would our faith be now?'

Ditmar wanted to bring Malcolm back to the situation at hand. 'But it is those Protestants and reformers who want to destroy the Pope. That is the battle we should be fighting – how will it help if you are taking Jews to safety? They were God's people, but now we are.'

Ditmar had had many such conversations with Malcolm, who never seemed to waiver from his inner purpose, something Ditmar did not have or want. He was habituated to feed off the bitterness he found in himself.

Malcolm replied a little more firmly, 'Our Lord had compassion on the outcasts in Judea and Galilee. We should do the same. Remember, God's foolishness is greater than our wisdom.'[9]

Malcolm went out to where Judah and Gezel were waiting, and arranged where they would meet in the morning. Judah would bring

8. Luke 10:25-37.
9. 1 Corinthians 1:25.

Kaleb, Gezel and Esther to Malcolm, and they would then go on their way.

As the dawn rose, Judah retraced most of the journey he and Gezel had made the previous evening. At a crossroads about a mile away from the monastery near Bernshausen where Malcolm lived, they met him. There he was kneeling by the hedgerow with a small open Bible beside him. He got up without speaking and acknowledged them.

Judah hugged Kaleb and Esther, and said goodbye to Gezel. The light on the horizon was gradually brightening.

'Come,' said Malcolm. 'Follow me. Tonight we will sleep under the stars. Tomorrow we will reach Hilders, where Gezel and Esther can stay, and you can then make your way to Amsterdam, Kaleb.'

Kaleb nodded in deep appreciation. He was about to speak when Malcolm raised his hand.

'The less we speak the better,' he whispered.

The horse and cart were heavily laden. The plodding sound through deserted lanes and narrow forest tracks was all that could be heard until a little voice piped up.

'Have we have come this way so no one can find us?'

'They know we are here but we are safe – if these farmers tell the authorities they have seen us they will have their own houses searched,' Malcolm said as quietly as he could, adding for Esther's sake, 'We have nothing to worry about.'

Gezel could immediately sense that Esther was not reassured.

'Why don't you teach me some more words, very quietly?' she said.

Esther replied, 'Give me your Bible and I will find a place in our Yiddish Scripture.'

Malcolm overheard. 'Would you like to use this German Bible?' he asked. 'I have a Protestant friend, a preacher, who has given it to me.'

Kaleb was taken aback by Malcolm's remark. How could a Catholic friar be friends with a Protestant preacher?

'May I ask who your preacher friend is?'

For a moment the need for silence had been forgotten.

'I'm sorry,' Malcolm replied. 'We are sworn to secrecy for each other's safety and for the safety of his family and my fellow friars.'

'Yes, of course', Kaleb replied. 'I understand. Esther, take Brother Malcolm's Bible and read Psalm 23 to Gezel. Do not shout!' he said, firmly.

Esther nodded vigorously. Esther read Psalm 23 from Malcolm's German Bible and then pointed to a word.

'What's that one?' she asked Gezel.

'Shep ... herd,' Gezel replied.

Esther proceeded to go through each verse, helping Gezel when she stumbled across a word. When they had finished, Kaleb indicated to Esther to give the Bible back to Malcolm, but she shook her head and hugged it close. Kaleb said quietly to her that she would have to give it back to Malcolm when he left. Esther nodded but Malcolm said nothing. He was pondering whether or not to leave it with them, but if he did, he was unsure if Kaleb would let Esther keep it. Still, there were an increasing number of Bibles printed in German which were in circulation and he felt confident his Protestant friend would find him another if he told him the reason he had given it away.

Malcolm seemed to know where the horse could take water. Streams were plentiful and they rested twice for bread and olives. Much of the journey was through forest tracks. Esther was enraptured by the sight of rabbits springing out from nowhere, and then suddenly disappearing again. Every now and then she would pull out an item of her mother's clothing and clutch it. When she thought no one was looking, she would take a surreptitious look into Malcolm's Bible.

She saw a verse in 1 Corinthians which said, 'My brothers ... some from Chloe's household have informed me that there are quarrels among you.'[10]

She looked over to Gezel and whispered, 'What does "informed" mean?'

Gezel thought for a moment and said quietly, 'To find out something.'

Esther pondered and then said, 'Who's Chloe?'

Gezel shook her head.

'We will have to hide the cart in the undergrowth,' Malcolm explained as the evening light began to lengthen the shadows.

Off the main track, they took some of the fallen branches away and hacked the undergrowth as the horse struggled to pull the cart over the uneven ground. Malcolm, Gezel and Esther pushed the cart from behind. After a couple of minutes, the path became too narrow and so they stopped and took the harness off the horse. Covering the cart with branches and leaves, they led the horse into a slight dip where they had cleared the ground sufficiently for everyone to lie down and sleep. After tying up and feeding the horse, they had some cold *kosher* lamb which Uncle Jacob had provided; they could not light a fire for fear of drawing attention to themselves. Not a sound was heard apart from the horse occasionally snorting.

Once the darkness had swallowed the daylight, Malcolm quietly spoke to them: 'I am taking you to the outskirts of a village called Hilders where I know a woman, Gertrude, who has been recently widowed. I think she will look after Gezel and Esther until Kaleb returns from Amsterdam. Her husband, who died a few months ago, was a candlemaker, but as the Lutheran Church has grown, the demand for candles has decreased. Making candles for Catholics is

---

10.  1 Corinthians 1:11, NIV.

no longer a respectable occupation. Now this widow is alone. Kaleb, you will have to pay her. You must go with her to the Lutheran church and fit in with their worship and take communion in both kinds. Keep the Bible and read it – Esther will help you, Gezel – for you will have to show understanding of their faith. Gezel, you must say that you are the servant employed to look after Esther, and will travel on to Amsterdam when Kaleb returns – just say he is a cloth trader. And say that I, Malcolm, have brought you there; they know who I am. I trust God that he will keep you safe.'

Kaleb and Gezel took it in, staring silently into the night. The flickering light from the moon through the shivering leaves, gently moving with the breeze, was the only light.

Malcolm looked at Gezel and said very quietly, 'It would help me to know your story so I can tell the widow why you are with Kaleb and his daughter.'

'I was an orphan but fled and lived an immoral life. Yes, I was a prostitute,' began Gezel. 'I discovered that my mother was the abbess. I now know she had no choice but to bear me so her father's rent could be paid. It turns out the priest who the Protestant soldiers murdered was my father.

'Something changed inside me and I wanted to see if my mother would accept me as a servant at the abbey. She did, but then a sermon against immorality was preached and I had to leave for my mother's and the other Sisters' safety. You know Kaleb had to flee because he is Jewish? He needed someone to look after Esther.'

Gezel felt a strange sense of exhilaration in being able to recount her story without being derided by her listeners, even though she had no idea what they were thinking.

Kaleb lay down. He could see the shape of the horse above him. Grief, fear and his life in pieces except for Esther, he could not sleep deeply despite his exhaustion. When he opened his eyes in the morning it felt as if someone had banged him on the head.

Malcolm was the first to rise, and quietly prayed and read his Latin Bible. Late in the afternoon they reached the outskirts of Hilders. Malcolm went into the small house which was set apart from the nearby cottages. There was a workshop at the back. Gertrude, the widow, did not smile as Kaleb, Gezel and Esther came in.

'Brother Malcolm has told me that the girl and the child will stay here,' Gertrude said, without expressing any indication as to whether she would be glad of company or not. 'When will you return and how much can you pay?' she asked Kaleb.

'If I leave you twelve ducats, I hope that will be sufficient for when I return in three to four weeks. May we also leave the cart and our belongings in your workshop, if you please?'

Gertrude nodded and went on to explain that Gezel and Esther would need to attend church with her. She would no doubt be receiving a visit from the pastor in the next few days. They would need to learn the Lord's Prayer in German to recite to him. They were to show no trace of being Catholic or Jewish. Esther's hair would have to be cut short so it would look as plain as it could. On hearing that, Esther looked at the floor. Gertrude asked them to all wait in the workshop after they had cleared enough space, unpacked the load and pushed the cart onto its side against an inside wall.

Brother Malcolm went into the house with Gertrude. From a small box in the corner underneath a heavy log, which Brother Malcolm moved, Gertrude took out a small statue of the Virgin Mary, a small bottle of wine and some stale bread. Brother Malcolm said the Mass and took the bread and the wine. After ten minutes, the box was opened again and the statue, wine and bread replaced in it. The log was replaced, and the others were asked to come in from the workshop.

'Thank you, Brother Malcolm,' Gertrude said, as her face relaxed a little.

Before Kaleb rode off on the horse with two heavy saddlebags, he gave Esther a long hug and whispered something to her. His orange split-brim hat and square shoulders disappeared into the distance as Gertrude explained to Gezel what chores she would be required to carry out, and how Esther would be expected to help her. They were to speak to no one and refer everything back to Gertrude.

Malcolm prepared to go back to the monastery at Bernshausen with some food and fruit Gertrude had given him. He waited till nightfall before he left the house.

# 12

# Understanding the Scriptures

The local pastor visited Gertrude the very next day. He wanted to know who Gezel and Esther were. It was his perfect right to ask such questions, as the Church and the local magistrates worked in tandem to ensure that all their subjects lived according to God's purposes. He explained that he could not neglect such duties, otherwise he could be subject to divine punishment.

Pastor Hinrick's voice was a combination of suspicion and anxiety. 'Who is this woman, and this child, and why have you taken them in? We cannot afford to take in infidels. The emperor has recently made his peace with France, and so now he may turn his attention to the German principalities. We can only expect God's protection if we keep ourselves pure.'

Gertrude told the pastor that Gezel was a reformed Catholic, as she was, and that Esther's father would be returning to collect his daughter and their servant after his travels to Amsterdam. Pastor Hinrick stiffened as he realised that Esther was Jewish, and Gertrude seemed to know little of Gezel's history.

'All I know is that the mother died in childbirth and the master hired the servant to look after her,' she said.

The pastor sneered. 'They can stay until the father returns, but after that, they must leave. While they are here, they must observe the true beliefs of the Church. Any deviation and they will be ordered to leave our principality at once. Do you understand, Gertrude?'

Gertrude bowed. Immediately after Pastor Hinrick left, she told Gezel and Esther in something of a fluster to study the German Bible for several hours a day before the forthcoming Sunday service.

'I have taken you in because of Brother Malcolm's kindness to me, and because I am now a poor widow with no income, but if you say anything to make them think you are not devoutly Lutheran, you will have to leave straightaway.'

Esther looked through Brother Malcolm's Bible until she found a verse she could read. Sometimes the words were too long for her to understand. Then she found one: 'Where is the one who has been born king of the Jews? We saw his star when it rose and have come to worship him.'[11]

'So Jesus was a Jew!' Esther said in surprise.

Gezel knew enough to understand that Jesus was indeed Jewish.

'So why do they hate us?' Esther asked.

'It's because they believe Jesus was God's Son, and most Jewish people do not believe that,' Gezel replied.

'Was he?'

Gezel shook her head. Esther wondered if that meant 'no' or if Gezel just did not know the answer.

'So they hate us because we do not believe in Jesus?' Esther was about to say something more when Gertrude came in from outside and told them that they must understand the story of the bread and the wine. Martin Luther had told everyone that Jesus was actually present when they took the bread and the wine.

Gezel and Esther were nonplussed. Then, with Gertrude's help, Esther found the place in the Bible where Jesus took the bread and the wine with his disciples. After trying to read the story, Esther said, 'So, when Jesus had the bread and the wine he was actually there with his friends, why didn't they have some olives too? – so now when we have the bread and wine on Sunday, will he be there even though we can't see him?'

---

11. Matthew 2:2, NIV.

Gertrude nodded but added, 'Do not say anything about olives. Just make sure that you say Jesus is there if anyone asks you, or they will say we are all children of the devil.'

Later on, Esther privately asked Gezel how many children the devil had and whether there was a mummy who helped them get dressed in the mornings.

Gezel loved the openness of Esther's mind, and wished everyone could be like that. As she fell asleep that evening, she began to think, if only that spear had missed her father's heart and one of the other soldiers had stopped the attack! Could she ever look after Claus if she found him injured and dying on the side of the road? And her mother – she must find a way to see her again; perhaps Brother Malcolm would help her?

The Sunday service came and Gertrude took communion, both the bread and the wine – Gezel and Esther did not take it, as all new entrants had to be baptised before they were allowed to partake.

Esther dutifully said, 'Jesus was here even though we didn't see him.'[12]

The pastor looked down at her and said, 'You are saved by grace alone through the death and resurrection of our Lord, not by good works, but if you deviate away from that belief your soul will be in peril – do you understand, child?'

'Yes, sir!' she said, even though she did not know what he was talking about.

The following Sunday, the pastor looked down at Esther as she was leaving church and said,

'Child, how are you to be saved from your sins?'

---

12. When Christ said 'This is my body given for you; do this in remembrance of me' (Luke 22:19, NIV), Luther rejected the idea that the bread actually changed into Christ's flesh, which was the Catholic doctrine of transubstantiation. However, he fiercely rejected the idea that communion was symbolic and therefore concluded that the scripture meant that Christ was somehow present whenever communion was celebrated.

Esther looked up and tried to recite the lines Gezel had drummed into her, but nerves got the better of her. 'Don't be a Samaritan but believe in the resurrection of good works by grace alone!' she stumbled out.

Gezel immediately interjected and said to Esther, 'Say with me...'

Together they said, 'We are saved by grace alone through the death and resurrection of our Lord, not by good works.'

The pastor looked at them with disdain and shook his head as the next parishioner said thank you to him for his words of wisdom.

The following Sunday Gezel and Esther were baptised, renouncing the devil and accepting the Holy Spirit through baptism. Underneath her shawl, Esther held on to a button she had cut off from one of her father's coats. Round her finger was the ribbon that Uncle Jacob had given her. The ribbon brought her mother's smile back, just as Uncle Jacob had said.

# 13

# Endings and Beginnings

Kaleb woke with a pounding head; he tried to move his leg but something stopped him. Looking down he was manacled round his ankle by a chain secured to a post sunk into the ground.

Where was he?

He remembered riding west towards Amsterdam, and making a fair amount of ground for three days. Then on the fourth day a figure came running out into his path and brought the horse to a sudden stop. And then nothing…

Had another man come out and struck him from behind?

Kaleb did not recognise the barn or the fencing near the edge of the field. His money and some documents on his person had been taken. It began to rain; through the sound of it he could hear some loud voices, none of them familiar. He saw shadowy figures; as he took a closer look, they reminded him of the mercenaries he had seen around Schmalkalden. One of them came over to him.

'You are worth more to us alive than dead,' he said. 'You will look after the horses while we are on the march. My name is Claus and I am in charge.'

With that, he strode off. Kaleb was later shown where the horses were tethered; his duties were feeding, grooming and mucking out. At least he was used to tending his own horse. But his mind was elsewhere: 'Esther! What will you do if I do not come back? My lovely Esther – are you to lose your father too? Will Gezel abandon you?'

In among the horses, Kaleb found his own. He took a moment to stroke and put his arm round its brown neck. The affection between them was comforting. There was a gentle softness in the horse's eyes.

'They must have robbed me and taken the horse – but who are they fighting for?' he wondered. 'How could my life be torn apart so suddenly? First, Judith and the baby, and now Esther...'

The group would move on every second day, having taken the produce of unsuspecting peasant farmers, and sometimes taking the womenfolk for their own pleasure after eating their food. Like all soldiers, they treated the land and the people as they pleased. There seemed to be about twenty of them but Kaleb soon realised he was the only captive labourer. He said very little to any of them as he waited for an opportunity to find out more.

One evening a soldier came to the makeshift stable where he was shackled, and gave him a tankard of ale. His name, he said, was Tobias.

'Thank you... which army is this one?' Kaleb ventured.

Tobias replied quietly, 'We will soon be part of the Emperor's Army. We are *landsknechts* – we have left the Protestant army – it is falling apart – Charles V is coming back this way and we will join his forces in the Low Countries. We will try to seek out the emperor's forces in Cologne but if not, we will march on. We fight for whoever pays the most.'

Tobias said no more and went back to where the men had taken shelter in a barn.

'Why did Tobias give me the ale?' pondered Kaleb. 'And why did he tell me all that?'

The next day, disaster struck; Kaleb's horse went lame as they came down a short, stony, muddy slope. The faithful beast limped to the stopping place with Kaleb's help but the horse's fate was already sealed.

'You will have to kill him,' Claus bellowed out from the front of the march.

Kaleb felt the beat of life ebbing away as he looked into the horse's deep-set eyes as he limped on to the stopping point. The sound of the horse dying that evening brought back Judith's screams as she lay on the abbey floor gasping for breath. The haunted groaning eventually stopped.

At the horse's end, Kaleb quietly wept; for the first time he was able to let go. He was wary of drawing attention to himself; the tears ran silently down his face for several hours before he fell into the dark pit of sleep. Even sleep was torture, for when he woke, his suffering was waiting for him just below the surface. The agony of what might befall Esther could not be forgotten even in sleep.

Esther took Gezel to the workshop and there underneath the cart was a small compartment nailed shut. Gezel found one of Gertrude's husband's tools and forced the compartment open. Inside were ten ducats and a piece of paper. The paper was a map and a set of instructions. The instructions were where to find money in Kaleb and Judith's house.

Just before he left, her father had whispered to Esther to open the box if for any reason he was not able to return for a long time. She had shared this with Gezel.

Gezel knew enough to understand that Kaleb's house would have been taken over by Herr Von Kram's men. The ten ducats together with the money Kaleb had given Gertrude would be sufficient to keep the three of them fed and watered for some months if he did not return soon. A time would come when they would run out, and as the days passed the anxieties grew much stronger. Esther felt that something must have happened to her father, as neither Gertrude or Gezel said anything about him.

One day, Esther announced, 'We can make a loom from the cart!'

Gertrude was about to humour Esther when she realised what a good idea that was. There were tools in the workshop and they could use the frame of the cart turned on its end to make the loom. If the wheels and axle could be separated from the frame, they could then take out the floor. They would be left with an oblong frame; along the top of the frame single threads could be hung down, each weighted with a small bag of stones. The rough cloth would be made by a cross thread, twisting either side of each thread hanging down.

One of the local men who had been friendly with Gertrude's husband in the past helped with the heavier work. Esther collected stones and together they made small weights for the downward-hanging threads. They worked from dawn to dusk, and also made a smaller loom from the floor planks they had taken from the cart. They started to sell the cloth at the local market and began to think about getting a Saxony spinning wheel, so they could make their own yarn from wool fibres – much cheaper than the yarn they had been buying from the town.

One morning there was a knock at the door. Gezel was surprised to see Sister Mary from the abbey standing there. She had come to give Gezel a letter. She explained that Brother Malcolm had previously visited the abbey to let Sister Margarete know that Gezel was alive, and where she was.

Sister Margarete had asked Sister Mary to deliver a letter:

For Gezel

There was a man who claimed to know the whole truth about God. Without realising it he was telling a lie about himself – that lie was that he was superior to other people because he knew everything there was to know about God. And so, without realising it, he was claiming he knew as much as God himself.

He began to enjoy making others afraid of God; what kindness and forbearance he had in his soul gradually ebbed away. We know in our hearts that people who are kind and open-hearted create sanctuary for those who suffer as you and I have suffered. Remember the poor widow who gave a penny to the Temple; it was more than the wealthy and important could ever give.[13] It was the wisdom in her heart that mattered to God.

Some of our traditions are right, others are wrong; some of our beliefs are right, others are wrong, and for those things men have fought and killed each other – we are all blind, we are all broken and we are all lost – we call on God to find us, forgive us and lead us. Can we not live with each other's traditions? Why are we so angry with each other? When we let go of the chains inside our own hearts, the resentments, the bitterness and the gall, as Christ did on this earth, then we might see a glimmer of hope. We are already in purgatory; it is the way out we are looking for. Keep looking, Gezel, and may God help you find it. It has taken me my whole life to realise that Christ suffers with us; it is that which releases us from a life driven by fear.

The main reason I am writing this letter before I die is to tell you that I treasure your forgiveness; it is the greatest gift God has ever bestowed on me. I will take it with me on my travels.

I love you.

Your mother, Margarete

Gezel had no difficulty in reading the letter. Those three words, 'I love you' meant more to her than anything she had ever experienced. Gezel saw that she had not signed it 'Sister Margarete' but 'Your mother'. And tears rolled down Gezel's face as Sister Mary gently told

---

13.   Mark 12:41-44.

her that her mother had died peacefully ten days ago. She was given her last rites and buried two days after her passing next to Brother Wilhelm.

———•————•———◆———•————•———

Tobias watched as Claus hit a man about the head with a stick, leaving him for dead as he ravaged the poor man's wife. Tobias turned away and realised that the man and his wife were much the same age as his parents, who he had not seen for three years.

'What would I do if it were my parents Claus was butchering?' he thought to himself. 'Would I stand by and watch my mother being raped?'

He had resented his life as a mercenary for some time. Secretly he would talk to Kaleb when he took him food or ale, and gradually he discovered that Kaleb knew Gezel. He thought back to the tavern where he had told Stephan the story while Claus had his fifteen minutes with her upstairs. How differently he now felt; then, he wanted to show off to Claus, who wanted to use people for his own pleasure, a pleasure that involved brutalising them. Now, at last, he could see what they were doing was wrong; he no longer wanted to be the callous person he had become. But if he were to escape, he would have to kill Claus. If, as everyone thought, Charles V's army would soon retake Lutheran lands, then Claus would return . . . and take Tobias' desertion personally.

One night, all the soldiers got drunk, except Tobias, who feigned his inebriation. As Claus and the others lay in their deep sleep, Tobias took his Katzbalger[14] and quickly slit Claus' wrist. Claus stirred, but not enough to wake, slumping back onto his bed of straw. By the morning the straw would be red.

Leading two horses out quietly, Tobias and Kaleb escaped.

———•————•———◆———•————•———

14. A small sharp sword.

Three days later Kaleb was a mile away from Gertrude's house while Tobias travelled on in search of his parents.

Kaleb came in quietly and Esther ran into his arms. He was gaunt, unshaven and exhausted, but he was alive.

On their journey back, Tobias had told Kaleb that many soldiers were mobilising in anticipation of a conflict between the Holy Roman Emperor and the Lutheran princes; travellers were even more at risk than when Kaleb was first kidnapped. Quickly and quietly, Kaleb decided to 'convert' for Esther's sake. What he said he believed, the religion he followed, his way of life: all of them had to come second to his love for Esther. She was all he had left.

Pastor Hinrick was in Gertrude's house looking suspiciously at Kaleb.

'Those who blaspheme against the Holy Spirit by impersonation will bring God's wrath onto all of us,' said the pastor, angrily. 'You were born Jewish, so you must be blameless in the sight of the Lord. Now, if you are baptised this coming Sunday, there is one more thing you must consider. You cannot live under this roof with a single woman without a betrothal promise, which must be carried out as soon as practicable. Otherwise, you will be guilty of fornication. If you do not wish to marry, then you must leave immediately with your daughter. I will give you one day to consider this. In the meantime, you must sleep elsewhere. I will return tomorrow.'

Gertrude persuaded Esther to go with her to the workshop to weave some cloth for her father.

Gezel and Kaleb stared at the floor in shock. Kaleb was first to speak. 'I can marry you in church for Esther's sake, but I cannot be a proper husband to you, because I have not even begun to think of how my life can go on without Judith. I am sorry – but please know how deeply thankful I am to you for caring for Esther . . .' Kaleb stopped and looked down. He stuttered.

Gezel interjected, 'My past – is that it?'

'Given what we have all just been through, I am not thinking about that. It would be a complete stumbling block in my own community – you would not be accepted. But that is not the point; my heart cannot marry anyone while I grieve for my precious Judith, and that will take years...'

'Yes – I do not know that feeling, for I have always been used by men for their pleasure. I do not know what kindness between a man and a woman is – I see only the bulging eyes of the men who have paid for me.' She paused and continued, 'I cannot replace Judith. Esther's grief for her is buried. When it does speak out, I would like to be there for her – it is, perhaps, the only worthwhile thing left for me to do. I cannot be a wife to you either, but I can marry you in church for Esther's sake and behave in public as a wife. You may not want that.'

Kaleb replied, 'Life is not what we want but what we do. For Esther, I will do anything.'

Gertrude arranged for Kaleb to sleep in a neighbour's barn that evening and on for eight more days until Kaleb was baptised. Two days later, he married Gezel in the Lutheran church. Pastor Hinrick did not smile once during the ceremony. The marriage tax was paid to the local lord and the couple returned to Gertrude's house.

That night, Gezel and Kaleb slept in the workshop, on separate straw mattresses against each wall.

As Kaleb lay down, he was left to his own thoughts: 'How have I got here? Where is my precious Judith? What would she say about what I have done? Here I am pretending to be a Lutheran and married to a former prostitute – what would our rabbis say if they knew? They would condemn me.

'But Gezel is kind and Esther needs a kind woman in her life ... will I ever be able to forget Judith enough to love someone else?

What would she want me to do? Can she see me now? Even if she cannot, her presence is real, just as they ask us to believe that Christ is somehow in the bread and wine at the communion service. I think I understand that a little. Thank God Esther is safe ... thank God ...'

Gezel, likewise, as she lay down on the straw, looked at the wall in front of her face.

'I cannot trust men, so why should I trust Kaleb, even if he can survive the sharpest grief? My life was wretched but now I have learned to live as if every day is my last. God? You must be so cruel if you are prepared to use men to kill people for believing the wrong things. How do we know? My mother was right – we are already in purgatory ... our only hope is compassion, not bitterness. Perhaps the purpose of her whole life was so that she could send me that letter ... there is, at last, someone who needs me for my own sake ... Esther.

'So what was the point of Claus' life? He had my body but not my soul ... I didn't know I had one, but now something has changed and I know I do ... now trapped though I am, I have to touch it and find it in the middle of the fight to live ... I will think of what my mother went through in that pigsty ... that letter is my life ...'

In the morning, Kaleb and Gezel worked on the looms preparing cloth for the local market. Neither of them wanted to provide material for soldier uniforms anymore, even though they had not spoken of it. They carried on as if they had been together for years. They knew they could live together as long as they did not become too close.

Esther, who slept in the house with Gertrude, would sometimes sneak out and take a look through one of the murky workshop windows. When the moon was bright, she could just see them sleeping on each side of the hut, usually with their faces to the wall – but not always.

Even though the twenty or so mile journey from Bernshausen to Rotterode could take more than a day when it was raining, Brother Malcolm now occasionally came to the abbey at night to conduct Mass. Very soon things changed when Charles V overcame the Protestant forces and Catholic authority began to resurface. Brother Malcolm began to conduct the weekly Mass as Brother Wilhelm once did.

Sister Mary, the new abbess, had intentionally kept one corner of the abbey free from images and statues of the Virgin Mary – she allowed some of the Lutherans to come there and pray silently. She knew they were sincere in their convictions and she had placed a Bible written in German for their use in the corner. The Sisters said nothing about these arrangements, out of respect for her; the villagers were very content to have the Sisters help them with the children, especially at springtime and harvest, and also when preparing the fields for winter. Sometimes it was as if nothing had happened.

Early one morning on his way to the abbey, after five miles, Brother Malcolm came to his regular stopping place. He prayed out loud as there was no one nearby: 'Father God, you know my innermost thoughts. What is it you wish to say to me? I feel unrest in my soul, but I do not know its source – should I fast or just wait here in solitude?'

He waited, reading the Scriptures and reflecting for as long as he could, but knew he would have to press on to be at the abbey before nightfall. He would take the Mass soon after he arrived and then after eating, stay at a local farmer's house before going back in the morning to take another Mass – two of the Sisters had been helping a local woman in childbirth the previous evening would return to the abbey in the morning.

After the morning Mass, Brother Malcolm was putting his Bible into the small bag he carried with him. Sister Mary asked him if he would like some cold meat and spelt bread to eat before he set off, and he gladly accepted. Although it was expected that Brother Malcolm would be left on his own to eat, Sister Mary sat down with him, for she had decided to tell him how grateful the Sisters were that he came to the abbey to take Mass. But without realising it, she found herself talking out some of her own preoccupations.

'Do you think our traditions are all equally ordained by the Lord God Almighty?' she said to him.

Brother Malcolm was slightly taken aback, but his inclination to reply seemed instant. It was not unusual for teaching to be given to women by men, but not through individual conversations like this one. However, it was the nature of the question that surprised him.

'God's thoughts are higher than our thoughts,'[15] he began to say.

As the conversation continued, it took on a certain symmetry; the balance between their belief and their uncertainty was similar. Suddenly the door of the kitchen opened, and Sister Mary was immediately on her feet, clearing up the dish Brother Malcolm had eaten from. Brother Malcolm got up equally quickly and five minutes later was striding along the road on his way back to Bernshausen. The conversation he had just had with Sister Mary came back to him almost word for word, and he found himself thanking God for Sister Mary's gentle spirit, knowing she was the reason for the unrest in his soul .

---

15. Isaiah 55:9.

# Key Contextual References

Robert Bireley, *The Refashioning of Catholicism, 1450-1700* (Washington, D.C.: The Catholic University of America Press, 1999)

This book explains that at the time of the Protestant Reformation, the Catholic Church was anything but static, with a whole number of spiritually based initiatives taking place. The constant shifts of power between Catholic and Protestant rulers leading into the thirty years' war after the period in which this story is set is also documented.

Maria R. Boes, *Crime and Punishment in Early Modern Germany* (London: Routledge, 2013)

This book explains the transition from medieval justice where reputation, torture and social status were key drivers to the Carolina of 1532 which brought in some procedures derived from Roman Law, using legal advocacy. The Carolina in itself did not bring impartiality into trials as vested interests were able to manipulate the outcomes.

John Alfred Faulkner, 'Luther and the Bigamous Marriage of Philip of Hesse', *The American Journal of Theology*, Vol. 17, No. 2 (Apr., 1913), pp. 206-231 (twenty-six pages),

https://www.journals.uchicago.edu/doi/pdfplus/10.1086/47917 (accessed 31.8.23) https://archive.org/details/jstor-3154607/page/n9/mode/2up (accessed 12.2.24).

This article contains the letter written by Martin Luther to Philip of Hesse concerning the legitimacy of bigamous marriage.

Frances and Joseph Gies, *Life in a Medieval Village* (New York: Harper Perennial, 1991)

This book gives an accurate perspective of medieval village life in England and Europe. It uses a case study of an English village in the thirteenth century in England to illustrate the work, family, religious and political life of the Manorial system.

Joel F. Harrington, *The Faithful Executioner, Life and Death in the Sixteenth Century* (London: Vintage Books, 2014)

This autobiography of an executioner's life in sixteenth-century Germany gives an insight into the social hierarchy, the role of the executioner and how they were viewed by the common people.

Andrew Johnston, *The Protestant Reformation in Europe* (London and New York: Longman 1991)

This short, documented history of the Protestant Reformation in Europe explains the contributions of the key theologians and political rulers, giving detailed references, dates, and citing key documents.

Benjamin J. Kaplan, *Divided by Faith: Religious Conflict and the Practice of Toleration in Early Modern Europe* (London and Massachusetts, Harvard University Press, 2009)

This detailed account of the extremes of religious bigotry and the practice of toleration shows how the confessional age brought about schisms within the Protestant communities across Europe and how toleration arose in the most unexpected places often for no obvious reason.

Thomas Kaufmann, *Luther's Jews* (Oxford: Oxford University Press, 2017)

Thomas Kaufman explains how Luther's initial sympathy towards the Jews (In 1523 Luther wrote 'That Jesus Christ Was Born a Jew') based on the hope that the Jews would acknowledge Christ as the Messiah changed into a vitriolic tirade when he wrote 'On the Jews and Their Lies' in 1543. Luther felt the mistreatment of the Jews was justified given that very few converted to Christianity in the German Principalities following the Reformation. He believed God's wrath was rightly being demonstrated by depriving them of their rights should they fail to convert.

Kenneth Scott Latourette, *A History of Christianity* (London: Eyre & Spottiswoode Limited, 1955)

This account of the history of Christianity includes a great deal of detail about the Reformation in many different countries, including Eastern Europe.

Martin Luther, 'The Estate of Marriage' (1552)

https://pages.uoregon.edu/dluebke/Reformations441/LutherMarriage.htm accessed on 21.4.23

This sermon on marriage provides a clear insight into the way Martin Luther used Scripture to explore the issue of marriage, divorce, faith, celibacy and the Catholic Church.

Werner Rösener, *Peasants in the Middle Ages* (Illinois: University of Illinois Press, 1992)

This gives an account of peasant clothing and food in the Early Middle Ages in Europe.

C.V. Wedgewood, *The Thirty Years War* (London: The Folio Society, 1999)

Although this book is about a war in the first half of the seventeenth century, it shows the deep inheritance of the political and religious rifts of the time the story in this book is set in Europe. It particularly shows how the common people were pawns caught up in the relentless territorial and theological conflicts of the period.

# The Historical Beginning of the Story

When the Protestant Church was formed in the early sixteenth century, it was not by design but through a combination of theological conflict and political pragmatism. Behind the headlines, as ever, were the power struggles among the elites which inevitably filtered down to the common people.

According to tradition, Luther (1483-1546) pinned a long notice on the door of the Castle church in Wittenberg in 1517. As a professor of biblical studies at the university, he wanted to state his position as to how indulgences, that is, payments to the Church, should be used. He opposed such payments being used by the Vatican for a new St Peter's Basilica. He believed purgatory was a reality, but thought any time spent there could not be reduced by paying money to the Church.

The long notice, called the 95 theses, was written in Latin, but without Luther's knowledge it was translated into German and subsequently printed and circulated widely. Luther became entangled with a much wider controversy than he had originally envisaged, and his views eventually led to a stand-off with the papacy. After some deliberations and attempted negotiations, Luther decided that the Pope was the antichrist and the resulting outrage meant that he would need the protection of Frederick of Saxony to save his life. There would be no reconciliation with the Catholic Church.

Frederick initially kept Luther in a safe house, not primarily for theological reasons but because he was keen to protect the University of Wittenberg, which he had been instrumental in setting up. However, the political context was much wider. Frederick also knew that Pope Leo X was relying on him and other German princes for military support in a planned crusade against the Turks. The Pope would also need Frederick's support in electing his preferred successor to Maximilian I, the Holy Roman Emperor. Even though principalities like Saxony (now part of modern Germany) were self-governing, they were also part of the Holy Roman Empire and Frederick was a formally approved elector who would have a say in who the new emperor would be. Frederick wanted his independence, but he did not want to cut ties with the Catholic Church completely. He had more than 18,000 relics, all said to have connections with the gospel story and various saints through the ages; Frederick derived an income from these relics, as their presence was seen as a source of blessing and visitors would pay to view them.

The Holy Roman Empire stretched down from the Netherlands through what is now modern Germany and Switzerland into Italy. It was bordered in the west by France and in the east by Poland and Hungary. It was an empire that supported the Roman Catholic Church, a Church which collected money in return for spiritual rewards, such as the weekly forgiveness of sins. Other sources of income were priestly interventions to allow a reduction of time spent in purgatory as well as rents and produce from its extensive lands. This pervasive corruption did not mean that the Catholic Church was devoid of genuine Christian believers. However, those believers had an even harder time once the Reformation took hold because of the polemic between the Catholic and Protestant hierarchies. There were a whole host of other smaller religious groupings which were offshoots of the Roman Church across Europe. The Hussites in Bohemia and the Lollards in England were two groups who had been pressing for moral regeneration inside Catholicism in the fourteenth and fifteenth centuries along with several writers, the most famous being Erasmus. Jews had settled in what is now Germany since at least half way through the first millennium; they were accepted by the rulers for the luxury goods their trading skills brought with them.

Electoral Saxony and Hesse, now parts of modern-day Germany, grew to become the heartlands of the Protestant Reformation in the sixteenth century. Luther and his contemporaries were in broad agreement that salvation was not dependent on the priesthood but directly due to the grace of God. They agreed on very little else, and fierce divisions centred around the nature of communion and the extent of the Church's governing powers. Whereas Luther supported the most punitive measures against those who did not obey the authorities, John Calvin (1509-64), on the other hand, became associated with a 'gathered church' which exercised total legal control of all aspects of a believer's life. Ulrich Zwingli (1484-1531), a contemporary of Calvin's, felt so strongly about this that rather than present a united front to the newly crowned Holy Roman Emperor, Charles V, Zwingli and his followers split away from the Lutherans after the Diet of Augsburg in 1530, a meeting Charles V had convened between the Catholics and the Protestants in an attempt to find a theological compromise.

It looked as if the disagreement would break out into violent conflict and a military alliance called the Schmalkaldic Defence League was formed to defend Protestantism. Philip, Landgrave of Hesse, together with Frederick of Saxony became its leaders. Not all of the German principalities, however, were fully behind the movement, depending on who their neighbours were and how their trade routes might be affected. Alliances were not set in stone, as they were always vulnerable to political influence, economic pressure and military threats.

However, frictions within Protestantism and with the Catholic Church were put on hold in 1532 as the threat of an invasion from the Turks increased. The Turks, in fact, could not give their full attention to invading Europe as they themselves were threatened from the east.

Potential conflicts between France and the Holy Roman Empire also diverted Charles V's attention away from a single military conflict against the Turkish threat. However, by 1543 when the story begins, Charles V was finally turning his attention to regaining the Protestant heartlands and the Schmalkaldic Defence League was edging towards war with Charles V's forces.

# The Historical Aftermath of the Story

Even though Catholic worship was reinstated in 1547, the Protestant form of worship was now established in every country in Europe with the exceptions of Italy, Spain and Portugal.

It would be eight years until the Peace of Augsburg 1555 pronounced that whichever confession the ruler followed, the people in his principality would be compelled to follow as well. Shared churches, migrations outside city walls for worship on a Sunday and covert churches were all attempts to accommodate the pre-existing religious variations within principalities. However, these accommodations were not enough to prevent the next 100 years being full of religious and political war across the entire continent of Europe.

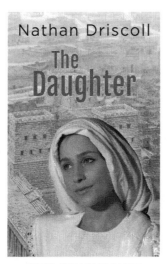

ISBN: 9781915046437

RRP: £10.99

'The Daughter' is set two thousand years ago around the time of Christ. A young girl, Rebekah, finds herself in a predicament – should she go along with the life her father and her Jewish community has set down for her? How much should she concern herself about the expectations of others? What will her mother feel if she takes a different road? If she runs away from the cruel man she is betrothed to will she just find herself destitute and die? Would it be better not to cause a fuss and make the best of it? At least she would have a roof over her head.

You can order 'The Daughter' at www.malcolmdown.co.uk

To order, scan the code below and enter code
**AUTH25** to receive a **25% discount**